THE
FRON

BOOKS BY SHALINI BOLAND

The Secret Mother
The Child Next Door
The Silent Sister
The Millionaire's Wife
The Perfect Family
The Best Friend

THE GIRL
FROM THE SEA

SHALINI BOLAND

bookouture

Published by Bookouture in 2019

An imprint of StoryFire Ltd.

Carmelite House
50 Victoria Embankment
London EC4Y 0DZ

www.bookouture.com

Cover image: ID 50045571 © Lasse Behnke | Dreamstime.com

ISBN: 978-1-78681-932-1
eBook ISBN: 978-1-78681-931-4

For Dan, my beautiful son

The dark water swallows me whole, pulling me under into blackness, dropping too fast. I cannot let the water take me, so I kick and flail. I push my body up. Water flows. Bubbles stream away. The sound of air and desperate splashes. The scent of damp night. And, at last, I see the inky sky once more. I don't have enough energy for relief. Instead, I gasp and thrash. All I know is that I must move my arms and kick my legs.

Keep moving forward.

Stay alive.

CHAPTER ONE

The scent of salt and seaweed. My throat dry. Lips parched. Head aching. My clothes cling to me, heavy and wet. Cold. Shivering. I can't think straight.

What's happening?

Eyes closed. A rushing, bubbling, frothing. Birds, wind, warmth. I cough, an echoing scrape. Painful. Everything sounds close by, yet far away. My body is stiff. Numb. I can't move. Can I?

Water rushes over me. Cold and salty. Like it wants to claim me. To keep me covered. But it seeps away, replaced by a mixture of cool air and warmth.

My eyes fly open.

A fuzzy brightness greets me. I see blurred outdoor shapes in beige and blue and grey.

My head is pressed down onto something cold and hard. Not a pillow. Not a pavement. Sand. Wet sand. Something presses into my temple. A stone? I raise my head with difficulty. And bring up a reluctant arm. My hand peels away a pebble. Tosses it aside with herculean effort. I cough. Retch. There's saltwater in my mouth. Bile. Tears. Snot.

Please, someone, tell me what's happening. I feel as though I'm trapped inside my head, unable to look outside. Like I'm covered in a membrane. Sealed in.

A muffled voice breaks through my panic. I try to latch onto it. But the incoming words slip and slide away – a flow of sound that I can't decipher. I try to keep my eyes open. To focus on something. But neither my eyes nor my ears want to cooperate.

'Poppy, no!'

A snuffling black nose and a wet tongue. A whine and a bark.

'Poppy, no! Come here!'

It's someone's dog. I still can't focus properly.

'Are you okay? I'm so sorry. Good girl, Poppy.'

I open my eyes once more and order them to focus.

'Are you okay?' The same voice, closer this time.

A face looms into my field of vision. I see a nose, a mouth, pink lipstick, glasses.

A noise comes from the back of my throat. But it's just a rattle and a rasp. Nothing intelligible. What am I trying to say?

'I called 999. Don't worry. Poppy, sit! The ambulance will be here soon.' A warm hand takes my cold one. 'Don't worry, you'll be okay.'

Will I? This person is here to help me. I know that much. That's good. I can give myself over to the help of this woman. I close my eyes again. It's too hard to keep them open. Too hard to focus.

More voices roll in and out like the salty water, like the breeze on my cheek. A wash of sound trying to break through to me. Part of me tries to resist the voices. Wants to keep them as a distant, blurring sound. Merging one with the other, like the waves and the wind. But a greater part of me needs to decipher the words. Needs to understand what's happening.

'Can you hear me?'

Another female voice in my ear. A younger, firmer voice. Her breath warm on my face.

'Hello, can you open your eyes? Can you look at me?'

I force my eyes to open.

'That's it. Can you tell me your name?'

Warmth spreads over my body. Someone has placed a blanket over me. I hadn't realised how cold I was.

'Look at me again. That's it. Can you tell me your name?'

I'm staring into kind brown eyes. A woman in uniform. Her hair pulled back in a ponytail. I open my mouth to say my name. But then I close it again. My mind has gone blank. It hurts to think.

'Can you hear me?'

I want to nod, but my head won't obey. 'Yes,' I say, even though no sound comes out.

'Good,' the woman says. 'Do you know where you are?'

'Beach?' My voice is a faint croak.

'That's right. Do you know which beach?'

'No.'

'Can you tell me how you feel, physically?'

'Tired.'

'Have you been in the water? Been for a swim in the sea?'

'I think I was in the water,' I whisper.

'Are you hurt? Are you in pain anywhere?'

'I… I don't know. Sore throat. Headache. Cold.'

'Alright. We're going to get you up off this sand. Get you away from the waves where you'll be more comfortable, okay?'

I close my eyes again. I'm scared. They're going to move me, but what if my body's broken? What if it hurts when they lift me?

The next few minutes pass in a strange blur. I'm lifted onto a stretcher. It's not as bad as I thought it would be; my body aches, but there's no sharp pain. People are watching. I'm awake enough to feel self-conscious. The woman in the glasses with the pink lipstick hovers over me for a moment.

'Don't worry,' she says. 'You're in good hands now. Take care.' She touches two fingers to my cheek, and then steps back.

And now I'm being moved. Carried away from the sea, across the sand. My body is still cold, but a warm breeze skims my face, the sun heats my forehead. I feel as though I'm floating. Light as air. The woman and the man in uniform talk to me, but I'm too exhausted to hear them. Their voices sway in and out, merging with the crunch of footsteps and the cry of the gulls.

The walls are toothpaste green, and the air smells of old socks and disinfectant. Stale and recycled like an overheated aeroplane. I'm sitting up in a hospital bed in the Accident and Emergency department, waiting for a doctor to see me. A nurse has already taken my blood pressure and temperature. The curtains are pulled around the sides of my bed, but they've been left open at the end so I can still see out. A teenage boy lies in the bed opposite, his mother at his side. I can't tell what's wrong with him. My thoughts are clearer now than earlier, my mind a little sharper. But my head still throbs, and I can't quell the panic in my chest, the constant fluttering in my stomach or the tightness in my throat.

Nurses stride past, calling out instructions to colleagues. Trolleys clatter as medical equipment is wheeled up and down the ward. At least I'm warm and dry. They took my wet clothing, and now I'm wearing a hideous blue hospital gown. I tense as I hear a woman's voice getting closer. Her accent is pretty, and I wonder where she's from. Maybe Russia, or Poland?

'The one from the beach?' I hear her say. 'How long?'

Another woman replies: 'Only a few minutes.'

The women step into my line of sight. One is a young doctor in a white coat, her blonde hair pulled into a bun at the back of her head. The other is an older lady, a nurse. The doctor looks up at me and smiles. The nurse continues on her way.

'Hello. I'm Doctor Lazowski.'

'Hi,' I croak.

She picks up a clipboard from the end of my bed and comes closer. 'How are you feeling?' she asks.

'Strange,' I reply. 'A little dizzy. I have a headache. I'm tired... and a bit freaked out.'

'Can you tell me your name?'

I open my mouth to answer, but, like before on the beach, nothing comes out. I give a small embarrassed laugh. 'I… It sounds so silly, but I just… I can't seem to remember.' I run a hand across my damp and tangled hair.

'That's okay,' she says. 'Do you know where you live?'

'I… I think I… No. I'm sorry. I don't know. How can I not know?' My voice is trembling and I'm on the verge of tears.

'You've had a shock,' she says. 'Just try to relax. Try to stay calm. You're here now, and we'll look after you. Okay? You have some retrograde amnesia, but with any luck, your memories should return soon.'

The word "amnesia" makes me catch my breath.

'I'm going to run a few tests,' she says, closing the curtains fully. 'We'll see how you are, physically, and then we'll try and get those memories back.'

I nod again, hit by a wave of exhaustion. My eyes want to close. I feel the pull of sleep, but Dr Lazowski is talking again. I should try to concentrate.

'Can you sit up, please?'

I do as she asks.

'I'm going to listen to your heart and lungs. Just breathe normally.' She takes the stethoscope from around her neck and begins examining me, first by placing the end of the stethoscope on my back. Then, on my chest.

'Can you remember swimming in the sea?' she asks, as I clumsily try to rearrange my hospital gown.

'No.'

'Were you in the water at all?'

'I think so. But I don't know. I remember lying on the beach, soaking wet. The waves were coming over me.' I give a shiver at the memory.

'Hmm, okay,' she says. 'We don't know how long you were in the water. I'm worried about a possible lung infection, so we'll have to keep you in for a few days at least. To keep an eye on you.'

'Is it serious?' I ask.

'Just a precaution,' she replies. 'We'll also get you on an IV drip.'

'A drip?' *I don't like the sound of that.*

'You're dehydrated,' she says. 'You need fluids.'

I close my eyes and massage my forehead with the tips of my fingers. What's happening to me? What am I doing here? How on earth did I end up unconscious on the beach?

Why can't I remember anything?

CHAPTER TWO

I've been moved to a different ward. They've put me on a drip to replace fluids. But the fluid bag gives me the creeps, hanging there like a grotesque transparent organ, so I'm lying on my side, facing away from it, staring out of the window at a flower bed in front of a wall. Thankfully, my mind is beginning to feel a little clearer – less weak and fuzzy – so the fluids must be helping.

But the dehydration and possible lung infection are not what's worrying me. No. The thing that's really upsetting me is that I still don't know who I am. At all. Dr Lazowski says that amnesia due to shock or trauma is usually temporary. She checked my reflexes and balance, and I also had to do some tests to check my thinking, judgement and memory. So far, it's just my long-term memory that seems to be the issue. But I'm going to have an MRI scan, so hopefully that will shed some light.

Truthfully, I'm struggling to keep my panic under control. My heart races, my head spins and I'm constantly having to wipe the sweat from my palms. How can I not know who I am? It's crazy. Surely, I should know my name, my age, my history. But when I try to find that information in my brain, it's just not there. The doctor told me not to worry. She said that they would try to find out my identity. That once I see my next of kin, my memories should all come rushing back to me. But what if she's wrong? They've been asking me questions every twenty minutes. Questions like, 'What's your name? Do you know where you live? What's your mother's name? What year is it?' And I always give the same answers:

'I don't know… No… I can't remember.'

All I do know about myself is that early this morning I was discovered by a woman walking her dog on Southbourne Beach, Bournemouth, Dorset, on the south coast of England. I've heard of Bournemouth, but I can't remember anything about the place. Do I live here? I have no idea.

I turn my head at the sound of voices and footsteps. The charge nurse is approaching accompanied by a man and a woman, both wearing suits. Are they here to see me? They must be. They're heading this way. Could they be relations? Friends? They look too smart. Like they're here on official business. I sit up, my head swimming with dizziness. I take a breath, try to compose myself.

'Hello,' the nurse says to me with a smile. 'You've got a couple of visitors from the police station. They've assured me they won't stay long. Are you up to talking?'

I'm not sure I am, but I nod anyway. She draws the curtain around my bed, all the way up to the window, before she goes, leaving me with the two officers. Both look to be in their late twenties, maybe early thirties. They're smiling at me, so I adjust my expression and try to smile back, not sure if I'm succeeding.

'Mind if we sit down?' the female asks, tucking a stray tendril of blonde hair behind her ear.

'Sure,' I reply, my voice a faint croak.

She grabs two stacked plastic chairs from below the window and brings them around to the other side of the bed, pulling at them with some difficulty. Her colleague helps her to tug them apart with a clatter.

'Sounds like you've had quite a morning,' she says, as they finally sit. 'I'm Detective Sergeant Emma Wright, and this is my colleague, Detective Constable Christopher Blackford.' He gives me a brief smile and says hello, before taking out a notepad and pen from his jacket pocket. 'Can you tell us who you are?' DS Wright continues.

I bite my lip and shake my head. 'I… I don't know. I can't remember. I'm sorry.'

'That's okay,' she replies. 'We're from the Criminal Investigation Department, and we're here to find out what happened to you this morning.'

'Criminal?' I ask, with a jolt of panic. 'Have I done something wrong?'

'Not as far as we know,' DS Wright replies. ''We'd just like to try and establish some facts. Okay?'

I nod.

'How are you feeling?' she asks.

'Strange. A bit weak. I've completely lost my memory. The doctor says I have retrograde amnesia… I don't even remember my name.' Saying the words out loud, I feel my eyes fill with tears, but I blink them back and take a deep breath. These people are here to help me. I need to tell them everything I know without losing the plot.

'What do you remember about this morning?' she continues. 'Can you tell us your earliest memory?' Her eyes are kind, but also focused and alert.

I think back to this morning, remembering my confusion and fear, like it was part of a dream. Disjointed and surreal. It already seems like a lifetime ago.

'I woke up on the beach,' I say. 'I was only half-conscious. Cold. The waves were washing over me, but I couldn't move. Like I was too tired and heavy to get up. Dr Lazowski said she thought I'd been in the water for a long time. For over an hour at least.' I shiver at the memory of the cold water. At least it's warm in here, under my nest of blankets.

'How did you end up on the beach?' DS Wright asks.

'I honestly don't know,' I reply. I have this nagging feeling I was in the sea, but it's not a solid memory. It's just an impression I have. But I couldn't have been for a swim because I was wearing clothes. Anyway, an early-morning swim doesn't sound like the sort of thing I would do. Even though I don't recall what sort of things I do.

'Are you hurt at all?'

'I've got a couple of bumps on the back of my head. They throb a bit, but the doctor doesn't think they're too serious.'

'Do you remember how you got the injuries?'

I shake my head. 'No.'

Her colleague is writing in his notebook as we talk.

'Do you remember anybody at all from before you woke up?' she continues.

'No, I don't remember anyone. Just the woman who found me on the beach. She had a dog, I think. Poppy. That's the dog's name. She wore glasses. The woman, I mean, not the dog.' I give a short, strangled laugh. I must sound like a lunatic. 'Sorry,' I add.

'You're doing really well,' the policewoman says.

I want to snort. Doing really well for a crazy person who washed up on the beach and doesn't even know her own name. 'I'm sorry I can't remember more,' I say. 'Dr Lazowski said I was wearing sports gear. Some kind of lycra leggings and top, so maybe I'd been running?'

'Yes, we'll keep your clothing as evidence, for now,' DS Wright says.

'Evidence?'

'Just as a precaution.'

A precaution against what? I think to myself.

'What time of day was it when you first opened your eyes?' This time, it's DC Blackford who speaks. His voice is deep and soft, and he fixes me with an encouraging stare.

'It was this morning,' I reply.

'Was it early morning? Still dark?'

'No. It was bright. I could feel the sun on my face.'

'Where are you from?' he asks.

I reach for the information in my brain, I even open my mouth to give the answer, but it's just not there. My mind won't cooperate. I try to conjure an image of where I live. Try to remember the place – a house? A flat? I shake my head and stare down at my hands. 'I don't know.' I realise my fingers are bare of rings. So, not married or engaged then, unless I lost them in the sea. Or maybe I didn't wear them for some reason. I rub my thumb over a line of callouses on the palm of my hand.

'Do you have any identifying marks?' DS Wright asks. 'Tattoos? Birthmarks?'

'I don't know. I'd have to check.'

'Okay, can you do that at the end of the interview for us?'

I nod.

'Can you remember the names of any people you might know?' she asks.

I look up again. Her face is open, hopeful. I so want to remember someone. But it hurts to think.

'It would help us find out who you are,' she continues. 'If you could remember someone's name, or even a nickname?' she prompts. 'Does any name at all spring to mind?'

Stupidly, the only name I have in my head is *Poppy*. This makes me want to laugh. I bite my lip.

'Anything at all?' the officer asks.

I shake my head.

'CSI went down to the beach earlier to investigate,' she says. 'To see if anyone saw anything. Maybe they'll find your bag, or purse, or phone. Something we can use to identify you.'

I nod.

'Would you mind if we fingerprinted you?' she asks. 'We can run your prints through our national computer, see if we find a match.'

'I suppose so,' I say.

'And a DNA sample?' she asks. 'That way, if you're not on our database, we still might get a percentage match.'

'Percentage match?'

'A match with a relative – a parent or sibling.'

I nod. Too weary to do anything else. I feel exhausted again. I want nothing more than to slide down under the hospital covers and sleep. But DS Wright is still talking:

'We'd like to pass your details to the local media, see if they can help us get the word out. Either to trigger someone's memory about what happened to you, or to find someone who knows who you are. Do we have your permission to do that?'

'Yes,' I say. 'Please do what you have to do. Thanks.'

'We won't release a photograph of you in the first instance. But may we take your photograph, in case we need it for identification? Is that okay?'

I nod again. I wish I had someone here to help me. Someone I knew. A friend. A parent. I don't want to face all this on my own. These things they want me to do, they all sound reasonable, I know it's all to help me, but it's still overwhelming.

The police officers ask a few more questions, and I answer as best I can. But I can't tell them any more than I've already told them. My mind feels like it's shutting down. Perhaps after a sleep things will become clearer.

The next half hour goes by in a haze. DC Blackford fingerprints me here, in the hospital, with a handheld fingerprint scanner. Then, he swabs the inside of my cheek for a DNA sample. They take my picture – I'm sure I look terrible, but there isn't the time or opportunity to check my reflection. I realise with a jolt of panic that I don't even know what I look like.

Lastly, I go into a private room with a nurse, and we check my skin for birthmarks or tattoos. Aside from an old, faint scar on my forearm, there's nothing. My body is smooth and blemish free.

I know these people are here to help me – the doctors, nurses and police officers – so why do I feel like Exhibit A? What if I never get my memories back? What if nobody knows I'm missing? What if I have no one? What if I *am* no one?

CHAPTER THREE

As I approach the hospital bathroom mirror, I'm almost too scared to look. Will I recognise myself? After the police officers left yesterday, I slept. Consequently, I woke up this morning feeling a little stronger, a little more determined. And I'm off the drip finally, so at least I feel less like an invalid. My memory is still missing, but I will get it back. I'll do everything it takes, starting with facing myself in the mirror. Hoping against hope that I'll recognise the person staring back at me.

I have deliberately unfocused my eyes. The mirror sits above the sink directly in front of me, but I must gather up my courage to look properly. I take a deep breath and stand up straight. I let my eyes relax and do their job of seeing.

Before me stands a woman – maybe early to mid-twenties. Sallow skin, brown eyes and a dark tangle of hair. She could definitely do with some mascara and lipstick. I put my hands to my face. To my pale lips, my dark eyebrows, to my nose which tips up at the end. I almost look like I could be Spanish or Italian.

Is that me?

I guess it must be.

Well at least I know now – my amnesia is so severe that I don't even know the woman staring back at me from the mirror. I am a stranger. I try not to let that information mess with my emotions. 'You're fine,' I whisper to myself. 'Your memory will come back.' I stare harder, as if that might change things. As if I can will myself to know my reflection. But the harder I stare, the stranger I look. My vision begins to blur. And without warning, I'm crying. I watch tears run down a stranger's face. I wipe them away with my fingers, but yet more tears fall to replace them. Who is that girl in the mirror? Who am I? Why is this happening to me?

I close my eyes to block out the forlorn image, sink down onto the floor and press myself back against the bathroom door, curled into myself.

Who am I? Who am I? Who am I?

I don't know how long I've been sitting here on the bathroom floor, but suddenly I'm tired of all the crying. My eyes raw, my throat dry, my mind weary. I tell myself that's enough now, snap out of it, and I struggle to my feet, shaky, but stronger.

I can't let myself think dark thoughts again. I must try to stay positive. Have faith that someone will claim me. Like a lost suitcase or a forgotten tombola prize with a raffle ticket taped onto my side. A hot shower will shake this negativity. It's only been one day. Maybe this time tomorrow my memories will return, and all will be well.

Half an hour later, I'm back on the ward wearing clean pyjamas and a dressing gown – clothes donated by a hospital charity. I must remember to thank them. My skin is clean and tingling, my wavy hair now thick and shiny. I already feel miles better. I walk past the other patients. A young woman stares at me, but most are asleep. I'm lucky to be right at the end of the ward, next to the window. It feels more private down here. I climb onto my bed, but sit on top of my covers, not wanting to lose the fresh feeling the shower has given me.

Through the window, I can see it's another clear, blue-sky day. It looks hot out there. I realise I'd like to go outside. Feel the warmth of the sun on my face and fragrant summer breezes, rather than this stifling hospital air. I wonder, can I go out for a while? I don't see any reason why not.

But a trip outside will have to wait, for I glance up to see a familiar face approaching. It's Emma, the policewoman – DS Wright. She's wearing grey trousers and a white shirt, her jacket over her arm, her face flushed. She looks hot and bothered, but she smiles at me as she gets closer.

'Morning,' she says. 'You look better today.' She sits, and pushes back a damp strand of hair from her forehead.

'Hi,' I say. 'Thanks. I do feel a bit better. I managed to get a shower and sort my hair out, so I feel more human.'

'Good.'

I look at her expectantly, wondering if she has any news. Then, I notice her colleague, DC Blackford, has also come onto the ward. He walks past the other beds, clutching two small bottles of water. He nods and smiles at me, passing one of the water bottles to DS Wright as he takes a seat next to her.

'It's roasting out there,' he says, unscrewing the lid and taking a long swig of water. 'And the air con in our vehicle has decided to pack up.'

I make a sympathetic face.

'Anyway, that's not important. How's your memory? Has anything come back to you since yesterday?'

I shake my head. 'Nothing. I don't even recognise my face in the mirror.'

'Sorry to hear that,' DS Wright says. 'But we may have some good news for you.'

My heart thumps louder as I wait for her to go on.

'I'll get straight to the point,' she says. 'Someone local reported a woman missing last night – a woman matching your description. We think it might be you.'

My brain takes a few seconds to register her words. I didn't expect them to have news about me so soon. I shuffle backwards on the bed and cross my legs, pulling my dressing gown tighter around my body. What am I about to find out? There are so many worrying possibilities swimming through my head, but I can't latch on to any of them. I can't think straight.

'Are you okay?' DS Wright asks. 'You've gone a little pale. Mind you, that's not surprising.'

'I'm okay,' I croak.

'The name of the missing woman who answers to your description is Mia James,' she says. 'Does that name sound familiar?'

Does it? I don't think so. I say the name in my head – Mia James. It's a nice name, but does it feel like my name? Maybe. I don't know. God, this is stupid. How can I not know who I am? I feel like the answer is there on the tip of my tongue, just out of reach. I grasp for it, but it eludes me. Slips away like a fish. Darting through the ripples to disappear. Suddenly, I'm tired again. My brain hurts. I need more sleep.

'Are you alright?' she asks. 'Chris, pour her some water, would you.'

'Sure.' DC Blackford stands and does as he's asked, passing me a glass. I take a couple of sips of the tepid liquid and put the glass back down on the side table, my hand trembling.

'Who was it who reported me missing?' I ask. 'Was it a member of my family? Or a friend?'

'We need to do a few more background checks on the person before we can confirm anything. But we wanted to run the name "Mia James" past you first, to see if you recognised it. See if it triggered any memories.'

'The name doesn't mean anything to me,' I say. 'I don't recognise it at all. Is that bad?'

'No,' she says. 'It just means we have to make sure that we identify you correctly. That you really are who this person says you are.'

'How long will that take?' I ask. I don't want to think too much about the name "Mia" until I know it really is my name. I'd rather not be disappointed if it turns out to be a mistake, or duff information from a crank.

'We can't be sure how long it will take. We'll process things as thoroughly and quickly as we can for you.'

'Thanks.' I'm increasingly curious about the person who's come forward. I wish they could tell me who it is.

'Your details are already on our social media network. They'll also be going out in the local press and on the local news channels today,' DS Wright adds. 'So, if this missing-person lead turns out to be a dead end, I'm hopeful we'll get a strong response from the media coverage. We haven't released your photograph yet. We'll keep that back in case we need to use it later.'

I think about the newspapers running my story today, about the local TV news presenters talking about "a woman washed up on the beach". It makes me want to pull the bed covers over my head and hide.

'I know it's overwhelming,' DS Wright says, almost reading my thoughts. 'But, you don't need to worry or do anything for now. Just rest, while we get the wheels in motion. We'll find out who you are, okay?'

I nod, grateful for her kind words, but also wishing they'd go now and leave me in peace. This is all too much. I really need to sleep again.

When they finally do leave and I'm able to close my eyes, all I can think about is the name "Mia James", and whether or not it belongs to me.

CHAPTER FOUR

I soften my gaze against the glare of harsh hospital lights, and wrinkle my nose at the sharp smell of disinfectant, so strong I can taste it at the back of my throat. My whole body pulses with nerves as I lie here on the scanner table, my head secured in some kind of cradle. I opted not to listen to music, so instead I'm wearing earplugs, and all I can hear is the blood whooshing through my body and thud of my heartbeats. Occasionally, the radiographer's voice breaks through this muffled seclusion, as he issues instructions and reassurances through my earplugs.

This is my third day in the hospital and so far each day has thrown up a new challenge. Because I had a couple of bumps to the back of my head, and because of the amnesia, they're using this magnetic resonance imaging scanner to check for damage or abnormalities in my brain. Dr Lazowski assured me this scan is "just routine". But everything starts off that way, doesn't it. It's all "just routine" until they find something; then it's not routine anymore.

I take a deep breath as the motorised bed begins to shift me towards the giant doughnut-shaped machine. My head will sit inside the hole while they take images of my brain. It's pretty clever really and if I weren't so anxious I'd marvel at the technology. But I'm panicking, my breathing heavier, less regular, my heartbeats racing away, the whooshing of my blood threatening to drown out everything.

'That's it, you're doing great,' the radiographer says in my earpiece. My hands are together, resting on my stomach, my fingers interlocked. My palms sweaty. I have this sudden, awful image of a crematorium, of a coffin on a conveyor belt sliding inexorably towards a red velvet curtain behind which lies a roaring incinerator. The urge to get up and run is overwhelming. *Think of something else. Think of something else.* My head approaches the scanner. 'You're doing so well,' the voice in my ear tells me. 'Almost there, and then we can start getting some images.' His no-nonsense voice jolts me out of my panic. I'm okay, I tell myself. They're just going to take some pictures and then it will all be over.

They warned me about the banging noise the machine would make, but even with the earplugs, it still makes me jump. It's a good thing my head is held in place. I concentrate on my breathing. I close my eyes and tell myself to let go of the panic. To think of something calming. This machine is here to help me. These people are here to help me. I breathe in, and out, slowing my heartbeats and easing my fear. The mind is an incredible thing – it can steer you to madness, or furnish you with comfort. I relax my brain and try to conjure up a restful image. I see water, but instead of feeling scared by it, I am soothed. I see dappled light playing across inky blue ripples. I hear a steady splash, splash, splash. Feel warm sunlight on my face. Is this a daydream? Or a memory?

The rest of the scan passes without incident, and before I know it, it's over.

I'm sitting on my bed, flicking through old magazines. I'm restless. Bored. I've been outside into the courtyard gardens. I've lingered in the cafeteria. Wandered the corridors. Been into the TV lounge with its endless rolling news. I thought I might have caught a glimpse of myself on television, but after an hour of depressing world calamities, I gave up and left the room. I'd like to wear some proper clothes. These donated pyjamas are making me think I'm ill, when I'm not. I'm sure I won't be able to stay here much longer anyway. I'm taking up a bed when I don't really need it. But where can I go? I have no home that I know of.

As I laze in bed, I watch the nurses moving around the ward, kind and efficient. Dr Lazowski says the danger has passed. That I'm no longer dehydrated or in danger of an infection in my lungs. Apparently, I'm now perfectly healthy. She says I should be fine. *Fine?* How can I be fine when I still don't even know who I am? I should have the results back from my MRI within a few days. Perhaps that will shed some light on what's happening in my brain.

The police haven't been back for a visit, so maybe their lead was a dead-end. Maybe the real "Mia James" has been found safe and well, reunited with a loving family. Or maybe she's still missing. I sigh, set aside the magazine and lie down. I roll over onto my side and stare out of the window at the brick wall, and at the flowers wilting in the heat. A gull lands on top of the wall. He fixes his eye on me and I stare back. He's big. He looks confident and sure of himself. He has no name, but he knows who he is. He knows his place in the world.

'Hello.'

I start at the words. Someone is here. The gull tilts his head and swoops away. I turn and sit up. It's DS Emma Wright.

'Hello,' she repeats.

'Hi,' I say.

She smiles. It's a genuine, warm smile, not a fake, polite one. It's nice to connect with someone. Even a semi-stranger.

'Mind if I…' She points to one of the plastic chairs next to my bed.

'Sure, go ahead.'

She sits down, hanging her black handbag on the back of the chair. 'I spoke to the charge nurse. She said you were well enough for us to have another chat. You feeling better?'

I nod. 'Still have no memory of who I am, though.'

'Sorry to hear that,' she says. 'We may assign you a family liaison officer – someone who'll be your point of contact with the police from now on, who'll keep you updated on any new developments in our investigation. But, in the meantime, anything you need, any worries, new memories, issues etc. Feel free to contact me. Here, I'll give you my card.'

'Oh, okay, thanks,' I say. I don't even have a phone or any money, so how on earth would I be able to contact her. She fishes around in her handbag, and finally passes me a white business card.

'There's a freephone number on there you can use,' she says.

I thank her and place the card on my side table.

'Do you remember me telling you on Monday that someone came forward to identify you?' she says.

I nod. I've thought of little else over the past couple of days. I realise I'm holding my breath.

'We've run some background checks, and we believe the gentleman in question has positively identified you.'

I digest her words. 'So… am I… Mia James?'

'Yes.'

I stretch my fingers out and take a deep breath. I feel the need to stand up. I slide off the bed and stand by the window, running my hands through my hair.

'You okay?' she asks.

I look across at her. 'Just taking it in.'

'I understand. It must be strange to finally find out who you are.'

'Who's the man?' I ask. 'The one who reported me missing.' I wonder could he be my father? Brother? Husband?

'His name is Mr Piers Bevan-Price. He's actually your boyfriend.'

'I have a boyfriend?'

'You do.' She smiles. 'We've done background checks on him, interviewed him. Cross-checked his statement with friends, your GP, your old place of work. It all checks out. You don't need to worry.'

'Okay. Thank you.'

'Would you like to see him? He's here, if you want to.'

A flicker of panic darts across my chest.

'But there's no pressure,' she continues. 'If you're not ready to meet him, we can ask him to give you more time. He's happy to wait until you're ready.'

That's a relief to hear. I can't deny how terrified I am to meet him. But isn't this what I've been waiting for? I can't chicken out of this. Maybe seeing him will help me get my memory back. 'I do want to meet him,' I say. 'But can you give me an hour or so? I need to... compose myself.'

'Of course,' she says. 'Would you like me to be here with you when he comes in?'

I shake my head. 'No, that's okay.'

'Fine. I'll go downstairs and tell him. He's desperate to see you.'

My heart is hammering. This is it. My life is about to begin again.

CHAPTER FIVE

DS Wright has been gone for almost an hour now. When she returns, it will be with my boyfriend, Piers. A boyfriend I have no knowledge of. A boyfriend whose face I probably won't even recognise. And I'm going to meet him very soon, wearing borrowed pyjamas and a dressing gown.

I'm perched on the end of the bed. The woman opposite is asleep, and I've drawn the curtain down one side of my bed to give myself the illusion of privacy. I glance up at the clock on the wall. He should be here any minute. My stomach buzzes with nerves and my body pulses with anticipation. I'm trying to remain calm, but the past few minutes have been unbearable. I should have agreed to meet him straight away, rather than allowing myself the opportunity to descend into a state of anxiety.

At the sound of footsteps, my stomach swoops, and I peer around the curtain. It's only one of the nurses. This is ridiculous. I need to calm down. I go and sit on one of the chairs by my bed, grab a magazine from my nightstand, flip it open and try to concentrate on an article about jilted husbands. I don't take any of it in, but at least I'm calmer than a few minutes ago.

'Mia.'

A man's voice. Deep and confident. I look up from my magazine. He's medium build, blond, tanned. Handsome. Holding a huge bouquet of flowers. DS Wright is standing next to him. 'Hello, Mia,' she says. 'This is Piers. Call me if you need anything.' *Good luck*, she mouths behind his back.

I nod, unable to speak for the moment.

'God, Mia, it really is you.' His face breaks into a smile. He strides over to me, lays the flowers on the bed, and opens his arms out. But I stay seated and lean back into my chair. He stops. His expression suddenly uncertain, his arms dropping back to his side. 'Mia? Are you okay? They said you'd lost your memory. But… surely you must know who I am?'

'Sorry,' I say, feeling bad for him. 'I don't know you. I don't even know myself.'

'Shit,' he says. 'Sorry. I was sure you'd recognise me.' His voice is clipped, confident. A voice some would call posh. Posher than my voice, I know that much.

He's dressed casually in shorts and a polo-shirt, but his clothes look expensive, his fair hair styled in a perfect French crop. He's also insanely handsome. Too handsome. Like, maybe he knows it. But I'm probably being unfair.

'Apart from your memory, how are you feeling, babe? Are you hurt at all?'

Babe? Okay. This is going to take some getting used to. 'I'm feeling much better now, thanks. It's been a weird few days.'

'I bet it has. I can't imagine. I've been worried sick, you know.' He takes a seat next me, and grasps one of my hands in both of his. They're warm, firm. 'You really don't look yourself, Mia. We need to get you home. Get you some pampering.'

'Where do I live?' I ask, wondering if he and I live together.

'Wow.' He stares at me for a few seconds, as though searching my face for something. 'I can't believe it. You don't even remember your house.'

'I have a house?'

'Yeah, in Christchurch. You own a townhouse on the river. It's a pretty nice place. You love it there.'

Okay, that sounds good. 'Christchurch? Is that near here? Is it my own place? Or do I share it with… anyone?' I'm too embarrassed to ask if we live together. It seems too intimate a question for someone I've only just met.

'It's all yours, Mia. I do stay over a lot, but you kind of like your own space.' He rolls his eyes and grins.

That's very good news. I'm glad I have my own place. I don't think I could cope with living with a stranger. Even one as handsome as Piers Bevan-Price.

'And Christchurch is only about fifteen minutes from here,' he adds. 'Not far at all. Can you really not remember anything, babe?'

I shake my head. He's so close to me I can smell his aftershave. It's a sexy, masculine smell, but it overwhelms me. He's too close. I wish he wasn't still holding onto my hand. 'Do you want some water?' I ask, reclaiming my hand, getting to my feet and turning to the water jug.

'No thanks,' he says. 'I've been drinking coffee downstairs all morning, waiting to see you.'

I'm not thirsty either, but I pour myself a glass just for something to do while I think about what else to say to him.

'It's been torture,' he continues, 'not being allowed to see you. I've been yo-yoing between here and the police station for the past few days. I've felt like some kind of criminal.'

I take a sip of water before replacing the glass and sitting back down.

'What happened, Mia?' he asks. 'Why were you at Southbourne Beach? You can tell me, you know. If there's anything you're keeping from the police, you can trust me with it. We tell each other everything.'

I look at him. Really look at him, for the first time. His eyes are bright, like he's holding back strong emotions. He almost looks as though he's about to cry.

'If I knew anything,' I say, 'I would tell you. But I don't. I really don't. It's like, everything that happened before Sunday morning has been erased. I have retrograde amnesia. I'm not faking it, if that's what you think. I wish I was.'

'No, no, of course not… I just… What a nightmare,' he says.

Then, something occurs to me. 'What was I doing the night before I was found?' I ask. 'Where was I on Saturday night?'

'Don't you know?' he says, surprised. 'Haven't the police told you? I've gone over everything with them a million times already.'

'No one's told me anything,' I say, suddenly wondering why.

'Well that's pretty crap of them,' he says. 'I would have thought they'd have given you that information. As far as I knew, you were at home that night,' Piers says.

'What do you mean, "as far as you knew"?'

'I mean, we were supposed to go to Rich and Annalise's party on Saturday night, but you said you weren't feeling a hundred per cent and didn't want to go. So you stayed at home, and I went to the party on my own.'

'Who are Rich and Annalise?'

'Friends,' he says. 'It was Rich's thirtieth. They had a party.'

'Oh.'

'Tell you the truth, Mia, I've been feeling bad about the whole thing.'

'Bad? Why?'

'I should've stayed in with you. I shouldn't have gone to the party on my own. If I'd stayed in, maybe none of this would've happened.'

'You weren't to know,' I say. 'If I said I was tired, then maybe I just wanted a quiet evening in and an early night.'

'Yeah, I suppose so.' He sighs and rubs his chin with both hands. 'But it still doesn't explain how you ended up on the beach.'

'Could I have gone there for an early morning run?' I ask. 'I was wearing sports gear.'

'What gear?' He snaps his head up and stares at me.

'Lycra leggings and a top.'

'That's your rowing gear.'

'Rowing?' *Does he mean water and boats and oars?*

'You belong to the rowing club,' he says.

'I row?'

'You could say that.'

'What do you mean?' I ask, detecting a hint of bitterness in his voice.

'You like to row, Mia. A lot.'

'In the sea? So could I have—'

'No, not in the sea.' He cuts me off. 'You row on the river.'

'Maybe I went out in the sea for a change… ended up falling in?'

'Unlikely. And why would you have gone rowing if you were feeling tired?'

'I don't know. I wonder if I'll ever find out. If I'll ever get my memory back.' A flutter of panic reappears in my chest. What if it never comes back? What if I have to start my life again, from scratch? With strangers. I stand up and move past him, edgy, fidgety.

'I'm sure it'll come back,' he says, his eyes following me. 'You can't stay like this forever.'

I'm not so sure. Silence hangs between us for a few moments.

'Shall I show you some photos?' he asks. 'That policewoman thought it would be a good idea.'

'Okay, yeah, great,' I say. 'Maybe I'll recognise someone or something.' I don't believe I will recognise anyone, but it can't hurt to look.

He gets out his phone and I return to my seat, scooching closer to him as he scrolls through dozens of pictures of the two of us together. We look pretty loved up in most of the photos. Leaning in towards each other. Gazing into each other's eyes. My hair is glossy and straight, my clothes figure-hugging and expensive. There are also images of our friends – happy, beautiful people hanging out in bars and restaurants, lazing on beaches, socialising on boats.

We appear to be a glamorous couple, living a glamorous life. A life that anyone would be envious of. A life I can't remember.

'Nice photos,' I say. But it's as though I'm looking at pictures of someone else's life. I feel no connection whatsoever to the girl in the photographs. No connection to this man sitting next to me.

'What does the doctor say?' Piers slides his phone back into his pocket. 'Can I speak to him?' He rises to his feet, a frown creasing up his good looks.

'It's a *her*.' I say. 'Dr Lazowski. She says my memory could come back at any time. That it was probably caused by trauma. You do know I had a bump on the back of my head?'

'Yeah, they told me at the station. Asked me if I knew anything about it!' He shakes his head. 'This whole thing is crazy. There must be something the doctors can do. We should get a second opinion.'

'Just leave it for now,' I say, not wanting a confrontation. I haven't got the energy for it. 'If my memory doesn't come back naturally after a week or so, then I can explore other options.'

'I still don't understand why you were on the beach. What would you have been doing there?'

'I don't know either,' I say. 'It's part of the whole losing-my-memory thing. You can ask me anything you like, but my mind is just this great big blank.' I'm trying not to snap, but I'm irritated with all the questions. I know he's only trying to help, but every time I'm asked something I don't know the answer to, it makes me want to shut down. Like it's my fault I don't know. Like I'm some kind of freak.

'Sure, sure,' he says. 'I realise that. Sorry, babe. I've just been worried, you know.'

'Of course,' I say. 'I wish I could remember. It's so frustrating.'

There's a moment of silence. Awkward. Piers is drumming his fingers on his knees, chewing one side of his lip.

'What about family?' I ask. 'Parents, brothers, sisters?'

'Ah, um, well, your dad died a few years ago, but you didn't really know each other. He left when you were young.'

I try to digest this information. It's strange hearing such intimate details about my life from someone else.

'Not knowing him never really seemed to bother you,' Piers adds, 'if that helps.'

'So, I didn't know him at all? Never even met up with him?'

'No. Sorry, Mia.'

'That's okay. It's not your fault. It's not like I remember the guy anyway.' I give a short laugh that could so easily turn into a sob, but I won't let it. I didn't realise how hard this would be. I almost don't want to find out any more, but I can't stop myself. 'And my mum? Is she still alive?'

'Yes. Your mum and sister still live in London. That's where you're from, but you moved here a few years ago.'

Okay, well that's good. At least I have a mum and a sister. I have a family. People who care about me. 'Do they know I'm in hospital?'

Piers stands up and runs a finger around the neck of his shirt. 'God, it's warm in here,' he says. 'Do you have to stay?' he asks. 'In the hospital, I mean. Can we get you home? Talk about all this when we get back? I mean, apart from the amnesia, you're fine, right? Things might feel more normal once you're out of this place. It's pretty depressing in here.'

I nod. 'I suppose I can go. The doctor says that, apart from my memory, I'm in perfect health.'

'Cool. Shall I speak to someone?' He rises to his feet. 'The policewoman, or your doctor? Shall I get you out of here?'

Should he? Am I ready to leave? After a moment, I nod. 'Yeah,' I say. 'Let's talk to them. See if they'll let me go home.'

I wonder if I'm making the right decision.

CHAPTER SIX

Piers drives me in his brand-new Porsche Cayenne. I may not remember anything about my life, but I know enough to realise this is an expensive vehicle. I feel mildly self-conscious wearing a pair of pale blue jersey shorts and matching t-shirt. They're actually pyjamas that Piers bought me from the hospital shop, but he said they look fine and that no one would be able to tell the difference. I'll take his word for it, but I do wish he'd brought me some proper clothes from home. Dr. Lazowski wasn't entirely happy about me leaving today. She almost glared at Piers when he requested it. But she finally agreed to discharge me on the condition that I come back tomorrow for a follow-up consultation to see how I'm coping without the hospital's support.

Now, as we leave the hospital behind, I stare out of the window, taking in the urban scenery, desperate to see if I can recognise anything. But it's all a nondescript sea of cars, roads and houses. Bland petrol stations and parades of shops. Nothing I recognise. Nothing I'm able to latch onto. The traffic is heavy. A heat haze shimmers up from the tarmac, making things seem even more surreal. Piers keeps darting glances across at me. I can tell he's worried. Uneasy. His attempts at conversation are wasted. I can't think of anything to say to him. Maybe this wasn't such a good idea, leaving the hospital so soon. I don't know this man, even if he is my boyfriend.

After fifteen minutes or so, we come to a prettier place. A small town centre with boutiques and cafés. Piers tells me this is

Christchurch. The town where I live. I sit up a little straighter in my seat, paying more attention to my surroundings. Although it's unfamiliar, I feel a little less tense, a little more relaxed. I think I might like it here.

'Do you live here, too?' I ask. 'In Christchurch, I mean.'

'I live in Bournemouth,' he replies. 'Not too far away.'

'Near the hospital?'

'God, no,' he replies. 'That area's a dump. I live in Westbourne.'

Up ahead I see a no-through road crammed with charming black and white shop fronts. Behind these quaint old buildings sits a beautiful old church.

'Wow,' I say.

'What? Oh, yeah, that's Christchurch Priory,' Piers says, as he swings the vehicle down an impossibly narrow lane lined with tiny cottages. The road becomes even narrower as the pavement disappears, and a family on foot have to press themselves back against one of the houses to make way for us. 'Nearly there,' he says, making a sharp left turn.

Suddenly the road opens up. Before us sits a huge grassed area with a traditional bandstand. Beyond that, a wide river teeming with boats and wildfowl. It's beautiful. Like something out of a picture book.

'Is this where I live?' I ask.

'On the quay, yeah. We're about ten seconds away from your pad. Or we would be if it wasn't for these idiots.' Piers has had to slow right down to make way for several groups of people who are ambling along in the middle of the road. 'Tourists,' Piers grumbles. 'They don't seem to realise that roads are for cars. It's always a nightmare getting to your place in the summer.'

My nerves lessen as I soak up our surroundings. The sunshine, the people on the green, the boats on the river, the swans and ducks. Restaurants and cafés. It really is picture perfect. Especially after the drab, sterile hospital ward.

Piers turns left into a lane made up of cobblestones. It doesn't look like a road you should be allowed to drive on, and there are even more people down here to negotiate our way around. We pass an outdoor art exhibition in the grounds of an old mill house. Directly after this, Piers turns right and we drive across a small bridge leading into what appears to be a private residential complex.

'I live here?'

'You do.'

I gaze at the row of riverfront properties as we cruise past. Three and four-storey townhouses with parking underneath and their own moorings. Piers swings the Porsche into a parking bay next to a pale blue Mini Cooper.

'Home,' he says. 'And that's your Mini, in case you were wondering.'

I gaze up at the narrow white building. Now we're here, my nerves have resurfaced with a vengeance. Although this place is spectacular, I still don't recognise any of it. And I can't shake the feeling that this must be a joke, or some kind of elaborate hoax. That Piers, and the house, and this pretty town in the sunshine will all disappear in a puff of smoke, and I will be left alone on a cold beach with nothing and no one.

He turns off the engine, its soft thrum replaced by the gurgle and splash of the river, the screech and squawk of waterfowl, the boat masts clanking, the shouts and laughter of children in the distance. None of it familiar.

'Here,' Piers says, handing me something. I look down at my hand to see a set of keys. 'They're mine,' he says. 'You've got a spare set in the kitchen drawer.'

'Thanks.'

'But you'll need to change the locks, babe,' he says. 'I guess you must have lost your keys along with your phone and stuff.'

I nod, wrapping my fingers around the cold keys.

'Shall we?' He opens his car door.

As I open mine, a wall of heat hits me, along with the damp smell of the river, mixed with diesel oil and barbeques. I follow Piers to what must be my front door. He's waiting for me to open it, but instead, I hand him back the keys, too disorientated to even attempt unlocking it. He does the honours and I follow him into a cool, dim entrance hall. I watch as he disables the alarm. 'I'll give you the code later,' he says.

'I must have a good job to afford this place,' I say.

'Actually, you're not working at the moment.'

'What?' I stop in my tracks. 'How come? What do I normally do?'

'You used to be a primary school teacher.'

'"Used to be?" Why aren't I working now? How come I can afford to live here? Teachers don't get paid that much, surely.'

'Let's talk about all that later,' he says.

There are so many questions flailing around in my head that I'm getting brain-ache again. He's already halfway up the stairs, but I'm curious about the rooms down here. 'Piers, what's in there?' I point to a door ahead of me.

He stops and turns. 'That's your office. It opens onto the garden. Well, I say "garden", it's really just a courtyard. The other door leads to the garage, and there's a loo through there. Do you want to see?'

'That's okay, I'll look later.' I follow him up the stairs to the first floor, expecting to see a kitchen or a lounge.

'Your bedroom, and a spare bedroom,' Piers says, pointing at two doors off the landing through which I glimpse cream carpets and plump, cushion-strewn beds.

He continues on up to the second floor. I follow dutifully behind. When he reaches the top, he turns and catches hold of my hand. 'Welcome home, Mia. I missed you.' He pulls me towards him and leans in to kiss me.

I jerk back and turn my head so his kiss grazes my ear.

'Mia…' he says. 'I…'

'I'm sorry, Piers,' I say. 'I can't… I don't know you yet.' Even his name sounds strange on my tongue.

His cheeks and neck flush red. He looks angry, but I guess he could simply be embarrassed. He has to understand that whatever our relationship used to be, it's changed. He's not my boyfriend. He's a stranger.

I extricate my hand from his, and step away, turning to look at the room, trying to think of something to say that will break the tension. It's a wonderful light-filled space up here. One half is a sumptuous sitting room with a cream corner sofa, a leather chesterfield, deep cushions and a thick cream rug. The other half is an open-plan kitchen dining room. French windows lead onto a wide balcony with views over the river and fields beyond.

'Wow,' I say. 'That's some view.'

'It's stuffy up here,' he says, pulling at the neck of his polo-shirt. 'I'll let some air in.' Piers strides over to the doors and tugs them open. A warm breeze winds its way over to me. 'Glass of vino?' he asks.

Good, we're going to ignore the awkward kiss. That's fine by me. 'Sounds good,' I say, relieved. I take a couple of steps toward the open doors, enjoying the cooler air. I desperately want to change out of these horrid pyjamas. I'm also craving a shower. To be honest, I wish Piers would just leave. I need to get my bearings and be alone for a while. How can I phrase it without sounding rude and ungrateful?

He strolls over to the kitchen area where he takes a couple of glasses from a cupboard and places them on the black marble counter top. I watch as he expertly opens a bottle of red wine. His eyes are focused on what he's doing, he doesn't look up at me once.

Okay, I decide, we'll have one glass of wine together and then I'll ask him to give me some space.

The night air is warm with hardly a breeze. A pearl of sweat trickles down my back. The river is quiet, the wooden building looms, its blank windows gazing at me, menacing. No one is here. It's just me, so why is my heart beating so fast, why am I so on edge? I'm waiting for something, for someone. And then I see her in the distance. She's walking towards me, unhurried, along the river's edge. I cannot run. I cannot move. She's coming for me, with hatred burning in her eyes.

CHAPTER SEVEN

I finally got rid of Piers last night. That sounds uncharitable, but I was desperate to be alone and he hung around for ages. He wanted to stay the night in the spare room – to make sure I was okay. But I managed to persuade him that I would be fine on my own. That I needed some space after the hospital with its endless parade of nurses, doctors and police officers. That I just wanted some peace and quiet. He wasn't happy about leaving, but I promised we'd meet for lunch today, and that seemed to appease him.

Now, I lie beneath the warmth of my quilt, my bedroom shrouded in darkness. The illuminated numbers of my bedside clock say 7.22 am. I stretch, slide out of bed, draw back the heavy cream curtains, and squint as golden sunlight floods the room. Once again, I'm taken aback by the view. Like the lounge upstairs, this room also has a balcony overlooking the river. I certainly knew what I was doing when I bought this place.

It feels luxurious to be here all alone. Like I can finally breathe. I may not know who I am, but at least I have my own place in a beautiful spot. I can work on the rest of it. I even managed to sleep well last night. My bed is so comfortable and large compared to the one in the hospital. I sit back on the rumpled quilt and stare out at the pale blue sky and the glistening water.

As my mind relaxes, a memory hovers around my subconscious. I don't dare breathe for fear of dislodging it. I wonder is it a memory? Or is it simply the remnants of a dream I had last night?

I'm getting snippets of feelings, but I can't seem to hold onto them. Desperately, I struggle to remember the details:

I was standing by a wooden building at night. But it was locked up. Deserted. I felt… scared? What else? My heart begins to thud as I recall feelings of fear. The image of a woman flashes into my mind. I can't picture her face clearly, but she was coming towards me. She meant to do me harm. I felt terror. I was rooted to the spot, unable to run.

I close my eyes and try to squeeze some more details out. But the harder I try, the more the details elude me. The feelings it conjured up are already slipping away. If only I knew whether or not it actually is a memory. It could just as easily have been a dream. How can I tell? I'm sure I used to know the difference between a dream and a memory, but my mind is jumbled, broken. Another beat of fear sounds in my chest, and I try to shake it loose, to recapture my earlier waking moments of peace. But that peace is shattered, replaced by deep unease.

I can't live like this. Not knowing who I am. Not knowing what is real and what is imagined. I sigh. It feels as though even the sunshine is mocking me. Everyone out there knows who they are. They know their place in the world. Yet I am untethered. Adrift.

I refuse to sit here and wallow. I'll get dressed and keep myself busy. Anyway, I have my follow-up doctor's appointment this morning with Dr Lazowski. I take a deep breath and wonder if there's anything in the kitchen for breakfast. Hunger galvanises me up and into the shower.

Fifteen minutes later, I slide open one of the doors to the wardrobe which lines one wall of my room. It's stuffed with clothes and shoes, and I'm overwhelmed with the choice of what to wear. Not jeans – it's far too hot. In the end, after rejecting several items on the basis that they're too glamorous, I settle on a chambray knee-length sundress.

Accompanied by my gurgling stomach, I take the stairs up to the kitchen, hoping there's something edible. There are a few tins and packets in the cupboards, but the contents of the fridge are more promising, with some salad items, Greek yoghurt, and a punnet of fresh berries. Although, I almost gag when I sniff the milk which is way past its sell-by-date.

Moments later, I'm heading out onto the balcony with a cup of herbal tea and a bowl of granola and yoghurt. It's more of a wide terrace than a balcony, with plenty of space for the two sun loungers and a rattan patio set which comprises a sofa and two armchairs furnished with cushions. I slide past the glass-topped coffee table and settle myself onto the sofa, putting my mug and bowl on the table with a clink.

A car engine starts up below. And then another. I guess it's around the time when people are leaving for work. Piers still hasn't told me why I'm not working. How can I afford to pay the mortgage if I don't have any money coming in? I'll have to quiz him some more at lunchtime today.

Through the balcony railings, I see a heavyset man in a suit, with a bicycle, standing in next door's driveway. He's talking to a woman. Arguing. Words float up – fragments of sentences – 'not my fault'… 'don't forget to'… 'No, don't be stupid.' The man glances up. He's wearing sunglasses so I can't tell if he's actually looking at me, or at something else. He raises his hand. I guess he must be waving at me, so I wave back, feeling slightly awkward. The woman follows his line of sight and catches my eye, but her scowl remains. They must be my next door neighbours. The man gets on his bike and cycles away.

'Matt!' she calls after him.

He doesn't turn around, just lifts his hand and calls back: 'I'm late. See you later.'

She glances back up at me, her scowl deepening. Then she turns and disappears into the house.

*

It's not even eight o'clock yet, but it's already warm, the summer sun rising above the river and fields to the east. I think I'll let my hair dry out here this morning, allowing its natural wave to come through. In the photos Piers showed me, my hair was immaculate – dead straight, styled to within an inch of its life with hair products and straighteners. A reminder of the person I used to be versus the person I seem to be now.

I chew my granola and gaze out at the river, trying to let my mind rest for a while. To stop forcing it to remember.

Half an hour later, I make my way back inside, the cooler air a relief on my heated skin. My doctor's appointment is at 10.15 this morning, and I don't want to be late. I'm pretty sure I still know how to drive, so I'm going to be brave and attempt the journey on my own. I know I could call a cab – Piers gave me a large wad of cash until my replacement bank cards arrive – but I want to get back into the swing of things as soon as possible. Anyway, driving will help me orient myself. I need to get to know the area.

I find a set of car keys in one of the kitchen drawers. I assume they're the right ones, as the key fob is emblazoned with the *Mini Cooper* logo. I stuff some cash in a small leather shoulder bag and head downstairs, ignoring the swooping nerves in my belly.

Satnav gets me to Bournemouth Hospital in plenty of time and without any incidents. I find a parking space without too much trouble, get a parking ticket, and make my way into the main entrance, my low-heeled sandals clicking across the tarmac. It feels like weeks since I was last here. I can't believe it was less than twenty-four hours ago.

I make my way to the Neurotherapy Department, give the name Mia James to the receptionist and take a seat in the waiting room. After skimming a magazine for ten minutes, I'm called into Dr Lazowski's room.

She gives me a smile as I enter the small consulting room. I'm taken aback again by how young she looks – not that much older than me. I guess I assumed a neurology consultant should be older. Her window is wide open, and the sound of distant traffic filters in.

'Mia,' she says. 'Please take a seat. You look great. Much better. Sorry it's so warm in here. I've opened the window but it makes no difference.'

'Hi,' I say, sitting down.

'How are you feeling?' she asks.

'Okay thanks,' I say.

'Have you managed to remember anything?'

'No… well… sort of.' I flounder, still not sure how much to say.

'Really? Well, that's great news. Tell me.' She has my notes in front of her on the desk. Her pen is poised, ready to record my words.

'I don't know if it's a memory,' I say. 'It could just've easily been a dream. I'm not sure.'

'That's alright. Was it a clear memory, or fragments?'

'Well, I woke up this morning and it came to me as a feeling, and then as images.'

'Go on,' she says.

As I recall the dream again, my palms begin to sweat. Images of the woman flash up in my mind. 'It was night time,' I say, 'and I was standing near a wooden building. I remember I felt… nervous.' I decide not to tell her about the scary woman in the dream. I'm sure that she was part of a nightmare, rather than a memory, and it would sound too over-dramatic. Anyway, I don't want to think about that woman, let alone talk about her. I shiver at the memory. The more I think about it, the more real it feels. So I push it away.

'Do you recognise the building?' Dr Lazowski asks.

'No. Sorry. It's probably just a dream, anyway.'

'Mia, it's good! You're seeing images and you're remembering feelings. This is progress. Whether or not it's a dream or a memory, doesn't necessarily matter. Before this, you hadn't been able to tell me anything. So, I'm hopeful for you.'

My heart lifts at her words. I hope she's right. I hope this means my memory really is returning.

'I also have the results from your MRI,' she says. 'I asked the radiology department to fast-track the results for me.'

This piece of news instantly takes my mind off the dream. I don't know which is scarier. I flex my fingers and then cross my arms, waiting.

Dr Lazowski continues. Thankfully, she doesn't string it out:

'According to the scans,' she says, 'everything is normal – no dead tissue, lesions, aneurysms or tumours. Your brain appears healthy. So there's no reason why your memories shouldn't return. There's nothing we can see that suggests your condition will persist or worsen.'

I feel my shoulders relax at her words. Now the results have come back clear, that's one less thing to worry about.

'Thank you so much,' I reply, my voice barely a whisper. 'Are you sure?'

'As sure as we can be. I don't think those bumps on your head are anything to do with your memory loss. Retrograde amnesia is more likely to have been caused by psychological trauma – the shock of almost drowning, something like that.'

The rest of our consultation goes by in a blur. I'm hardly concentrating, my relief is so great. She gives me a list of things I can do to try to help my memory along. Things such as talking to friends and family, revisiting familiar places – old schools, places of work, clubs, usual routes etc. I nod along, and resolve to do everything she's telling me. She's also going to schedule me in for regular therapy and a follow-up consultation.

Although the results of the scan are good, it still doesn't explain what happened to me. I still don't know how I ended up unconscious on the beach with no memory. And, although I know my name and where I live, I still don't really know who I am.

CHAPTER EIGHT

After my hospital appointment, I stop off at home to freshen up before my lunch date with Piers. I'm going to walk to the restaurant which is somewhere in Christchurch. Given that the town centre is more-or-less one long street with a few little side roads, I'm confident I'll find it. I leave the house and head away from the river towards the Priory. I find myself cutting through a busy car park, weaving past queues for the ticket machine and parents wrestling with car seats and pushchairs. All these people leading normal lives with people they love – or maybe they hate, but at least they *know* them. The only person I know is Piers, and today I'm determined to get to know him better.

Leaving the car park behind, I find myself in the shadow of the Priory, walking along a path through a grassy graveyard. The gravestones are old and worn, covered in white spots and lichen. I draw my gaze up, and am mesmerised by the grand stature of the building, by its ancient solidity, its huge square tower staring down at me. I wonder how long it's been standing here. What dramas and tragedies it's seen during its lifetime.

Piers gave me directions yesterday. He told me I needed to turn right at the roundabout. I spot it up ahead, a little further along the crowded high street. Nothing about this place seems familiar. No landmark or shop that I recognise. I don't have any sense of having been here before, other than the drive home yesterday. Maybe, I'm concentrating too hard, too desperate to remember.

I'm hungry again. Haven't eaten since breakfast so I'm more than ready for lunch. A few moments more and I find myself pushing open the door to a pretty French restaurant. I don't know why I expected it to be half empty. Instead, it's buzzing with diners. There doesn't appear to be a single spare table. I hope Piers has booked.

A young waiter comes over and I'm about to give him my name, but he smiles and kisses me on both cheeks.

'Mia!' he says, with no trace of a French accent. I'm guessing he must be local. 'We heard about your accident. I saw all about it on television. How are you? You look amazing as always. Piers is already here at your usual table.'

I push my sunglasses up onto my head and glance around, not sure where our 'usual' table would be.

'Here,' the waiter says. 'By the window.'

I turn back around to see Piers smiling up at me. I'm taken aback again by how handsome he is. He also looks friendlier than he did yesterday. Maybe he was just more worried. He could've been nervous, too. I think I might have been a little harsh on Piers. He's my boyfriend, so I must like him. Maybe I even love him. I wonder what stage our relationship has reached. Are we serious? How long have we been going out? I need to ask him all these questions, and more. Surely, there has to be some connection or spark between us.

'Thank you,' I say to the waiter.

'Cheers, mate,' Piers says. 'Can you bring Mia a glass of Prosecco?'

'Sure.'

Piers stands and we kiss on the cheek. He didn't even attempt the lips today, for which I'm grateful. Maybe he has some sensitivity after all.

'How was the hospital?' he asks, sitting back down. 'You should have let me take you.'

I sit down and dump my bag on the window sill. 'It was fine. I didn't get lost once.'

'You drove?' He frowns and shakes his head. 'I told you to take a cab.'

'I'm fine, Piers. I'm not ill. Just a little... memory impaired.'

'Okay, babe. I'm just worried about you, that's all.'

'Thank you.' I smile, thinking how it's nice to have someone worry about me.

'So, what did the doctor say?' he asks, taking a sip of wine.

'It's good news, I suppose. My brain scan came back negative. There's nothing bad there. It's just a case of amnesia, and hopefully, my memory will start returning soon.'

'That's amazing news. We should have a toast.'

The waiter returns with my drink. I take it from him and raise it in Piers' direction.

'To memories,' he says.

I grin. 'To memories.' We clink glasses.

'I hope you don't mind, I already ordered for you. You always have the same thing anyway.'

'What do I always have?' I ask, curious.

'Wait and see.'

'That's mean!' I give him a fake glare. 'Tell me.'

'I see you're still impatient,' he says with an eye roll and a smirk.

'Fine. I can wait. I am starving, though.' I reach across to the basket in the centre of the table and break off a piece of warm crusty bread.

'Hmm,' Piers says. 'That's new.'

'What?' I say, popping the bread into my mouth.

'Nothing. Just... you never used to eat bread.'

'Why not? This stuff is heaven.' I tear off another chunk.

Piers leans across the table. 'You've got flour...' he wipes the side of my mouth with his thumb. It's an intimate gesture and I'm annoyed to feel myself blushing.

'So,' I say, wiping at imaginary crumbs on my dress. 'What is it you do... for a living, I mean?'

'I'm a property developer.'

'Oh, okay. So, you like, do houses up, and sell them on?'

'Pretty much, yeah.'

'Have you got any properties at the moment?' I ask.

'I'm working on one. Early stages,' he says, taking a healthy swig of his wine.

My drink has already gone straight to my head.

'Do you like it?' I ask. 'Being a property developer? Have you done it for long?' I tear off another chunk of bread and stuff it into my mouth in a half-hearted attempt to soak up the alcohol.

'Not that long, no,' he says, draining his glass. 'It's okay, yeah. Hard work, though.'

'Do you do the actual… developing?' I ask. I'm not even sure if I'm interested in what he's saying, or if I'm merely trying to keep the conversation flowing. 'Or do you pay people to work for you?'

'A bit of both.'

'And you said before that I don't work?'

'Not at the moment. You're taking a break from teaching.'

'Why would I take a break?'

'I… Oh, here's lunch.'

I look up to see our waiter returning. Piers has ordered the filet mignon with French fries, and I have a disappointing salad. I eye his steak hungrily.

'Duck salad with asparagus,' Piers says. 'Your favourite.'

'Lovely, thank you,' I say, wishing he had let me order my own food.

He orders himself another glass of wine and we dig in. After my initial disappointment, I find the salad is actually delicious, and also quite filling. It would seem the old me knows what I like to eat.

'I had a strange dream last night,' I say, taking a sip of Prosecco. 'But I'm wondering if it might have been a memory.'

'What was it about?'

'It's silly really. I was standing outside a wooden building at night.'

'A wooden building? What sort of building? A house? A shed?'

'I don't think it was either.' I conjure up the image in my mind. 'It looked like a massive garage. I guess it could have been a storage shed or something. But I think it had this huge overhanging balcony. It was by the river.'

'Sounds like the rowing club,' Piers says, spearing a French fry.

'Do you think so?' My heart gives a leap as I realise I could have experienced a real memory.

'I don't know,' he says. 'Maybe.'

The scary woman flashes into my mind. I stare at Piers' face to try to block her out, push her away. 'I'll go there after lunch,' I say, swallowing down a beat of fear. 'See if I recognise it.'

'Sounds about right,' Piers says, swallowing a mouthful of food followed by another swig of wine.

'What's that supposed to mean?'

'I mean, it sounds about right that you've only been out of hospital for one day, and you're going back to the bloody rowing club already.' He twists his lip into an irritated smile.

'What are you talking about?' I say. 'If that's my first memory, of course I have to go there. I have to see if it triggers anything else.'

'Sure,' he replies, draining his glass and signalling the waiter for yet another.

'You do understand that, don't you?' I say, annoyed that he doesn't seem to get it. That he's letting past issues cloud my current predicament.

'I understand,' he grunts.

'What's the issue with me and the rowing club, anyway?' I lay my knife and fork down, suddenly not hungry anymore.

'Nothing. Forget it.'

'Well, I can't forget it. It's obviously something that's causing a problem between us.'

He glances around. 'Where's that bloody waiter with my wine? I should've ordered a bottle.'

'Piers?' I try to get his attention back. 'Tell me, what the problem is with the rowing club?'

'You just spend a lot of time on the water, that's all.'

'Okay. Sorry, I guess. But you do understand why I have to go there today, don't you? If it could help me get my memory back, then…'

'Yeah, sure.' He scowls.

'Why don't you come with me?' I say, trying to revive his mood.

'Too much going on with the flat this afternoon. I've got the bathroom suite being delivered and I'm the only one on site today.'

'Oh. Okay,' I say, half-relieved he won't be coming with me. It's something I should probably do alone. If Piers is there, I won't be able to think properly. I won't be able to concentrate on remembering.

'I'll come over to your place later, though,' he says, brightening a little.

'Could we make it tomorrow instead?' I ask. 'I really want an early night. I'm so tired, still.'

'Just for an hour or two?' he says, wheedling. 'I won't stay long.'

It would be easier to give into him. He looks like he doesn't want to take no for an answer. But I know I'd regret it later. 'Not tonight,' I say. 'Honestly, I won't be good company.'

'Mia,' Piers says, pushing his empty plate away, and wiping his mouth with his napkin. 'Do you know how weird this all is for me?'

Weird for *him*? 'Um, yeah. Of course.'

'I mean, one day you're my girlfriend. You love me and we have a great relationship. The next day you don't even know who I am, and you don't want me coming over. It's weird, right?'

'Of course it's weird, Piers.' I try to keep my voice level, not quite believing that he could think his situation is any stranger than my own. 'I get that it's hard for you. But it's not something I've chosen. I didn't *want* to lose my memory. I don't know anything about myself. I don't know what I like to eat, what clothes I like to wear. I didn't even recognise my face in the mirror, for fuck's sake.'

'Whoa,' he says, raising his hands in submission. 'Easy there, tiger. I'm just trying to have a conversation about everything. Trying to work out what we should do.' He runs his fingers up and down the back of his head, massaging his scalp.

'Sorry. I didn't mean to snap. Didn't mean to swear.' I exhale and stare through the window at a middle-aged couple browsing the menu outside. Piers must think I'm a total cow, losing my temper like that. 'I don't even know how old I am,' I murmur.

'You're twenty-five,' Piers says with a sigh.

'Oh.' I guess twenty-five seems like an okay age to be. I look across at him. He's staring down at his empty plate. I can't tell if he's upset, or angry, or what. 'If it's awkward for you,' I begin. 'Do you want… I mean, should we… I don't know… take a break. Split up or something?'

'What? Jesus, no, Mia. That's the last thing I want.' He reaches across the table and takes both my hands. 'You may not know me anymore, but I know you, Mia James. And I love you. We're great together, and I'm going to make sure you know it.'

I suddenly realise that of course it must be awful for Piers. To have the person you love stare at you blankly, like you mean nothing. What a kick in the guts. I give his hands a squeeze, and smile weakly.

'Thank you,' is all I manage to say.

CHAPTER NINE

After my lunch with Piers, I'm all antsy and keyed-up. I'm walking back home, and feel like I want to go for a run or something, but it's far too hot. It must be 35 degrees out. Unless my memory returns, I really don't see how Piers and I are going to make it work. I don't feel any connection between us. There's no spark. Not for me, anyway.

A mobile phone shop catches my eye and I decide to go inside and pick out a new phone. Not that I know many people to call, but I guess I'll need one eventually. I spend an hour or so in there, and finally leave with a phone that's made the sales guy far happier than me. I step back out onto the pavement feeling hot and bothered, unable to relax. I'm still walking back in the direction of home, but I don't want to go back yet. Instead, I think I'm going to head straight to the rowing club. I'm not sure where it is, but maybe I can ask someone.

I walk quickly despite the heat, and now I'm almost back at the quay. There's some kind of sailing club near my house. Maybe the rowing club is part of it. As I walk back through the car park, I'm grateful for the shade provided by all the trees here, along with the hint of breeze coming off the river. I leave the cool of the car park and cross the cobbled road, walking over the stone bridge and heading towards the boats. There are quite a few people milling about. I approach a family who are loading supplies into a dinghy.

'Excuse me,' I say to the woman, who's chastising her young sons for mucking about instead of helping. She turns to me with an irritated expression, but it transforms into a smile when she realises I'm not a misbehaving child.

'Hello,' she says. 'You going out on the water this afternoon? Isn't it just the most perfect day.'

'It's gorgeous,' I agree. 'I'm actually looking for the rowing club.'

'Oh, okay. You're at the wrong end.' She points west. 'It's about a ten-minute walk in that direction. You can't miss it. It's just past the kids' playground.'

'Thank you,' I reply.

'Hot work, though,' she says, 'rowing in this heat. You must be fit.'

I smile. 'Thanks again.'

I leave the bustle of the sailing club behind, and walk along the gently curving river, passing overfed ducks and swans, admiring the silvery reed beds on the opposite bank, and a pretty wooden house which sits alone amid the long grass. I pass elderly couples relaxing on wooden benches, and families playing ball games on the field. Dogs trot lazily in the heat and children squeal with delight in the playground and water park up ahead. I'm alert for anything which might look familiar to me, but it's all fresh, new and interesting. Nothing to suggest I've been here before.

As I pass the playground and come around a sharp bend, I spot four teens at the river's edge, gathering up their blades ready to climb into their boat. Wellington boots lie discarded on the shingle, and their instructor is sliding a launch into the water.

I jog towards her, hoping to have a word before their session gets underway. I wonder if she might recognise me. But as I draw closer, I glance to my right and catch my breath.

It's the building. The one from my dream. Piers was right. Sitting close to the river bank, it's ultra-modern, clad in wood, with a floor-to-ceiling window on the upper level, leading onto a huge wrap-around balcony. It seems slightly different to how I remember it – bigger and more imposing somehow – but maybe that's because now it's a bright sunny day, rather than a lonely dark night, like in my dream. There's no doubt in my mind that this is the same building, though. My heart rate accelerates, and I stare ahead to the path along the river, expecting to see the woman from my dream coming for me. Of course, there is no woman there, just a family throwing a ball into the river for their collie dog to retrieve. My pulse slows and I attempt to get my breathing back under control.

Apart from the coach and her students at the water's edge, the club itself appears deserted.

'Excuse me,' I call out.

The coach turns and frowns. I don't recognise her. Her students are already in their scull, and she's seconds from following them. I step down onto the shingle slipway and smile at her, but she doesn't say anything or return my smile.

'Is there anyone in the clubhouse?' I ask. 'Can I go in?'

'Are you a member?'

'I think so.' As I say the words, I realise how dodgy they sound, and I don't blame her for the look she gives me. But I can't start telling a total stranger about my amnesia; she'll think I'm even weirder. 'I used to be a member,' I say, saving my faux pas.

'Oh, right. Well, if you want to renew your membership, you're best off giving them a call. They can talk you through it. You can find the details online.'

'Okay, thanks.'

'No problem.' She hops up onto the launch and motors off after her students who have already pulled away upstream. I stare after them for a moment, envious. Feeling as though I'd like to be out there, too.

I guess that's it for now. I should go back home. Thank goodness I managed to put Piers off coming round tonight. It's too much like hard work trying to figure out how our relationship should be. I'll have to try harder. I guess I owe him that much. Just… not tonight.

I should be pleased with how things have gone this afternoon. At least I know this building is definitely the one from my memory, so there's every chance more memories will start returning. That's got to be good news. But I get a strange vibe from the place. It's comfortable here, and kind of familiar, but it's also making my stomach flutter with nerves.

'Mia!'

I turn at the mention of my name, already becoming used to the sound of it. A man dressed in shorts, t-shirt and trainers comes out of a door in the side of the clubhouse. He brings a hand up to shade his eyes and takes a step towards me.

'Mia? It is you isn't it?'

'Hello?' I say, taking a step towards him.

'It's me, Jack.'

'Sorry, do I know you?' I hunch my shoulders and flush at the thought of not recognising a possible friend or acquaintance. He must think I'm so rude. I'll have to explain my amnesia.

He gives me a smile, his head tipped to the side in a gesture of sympathy. 'I heard what happened, Mia. The police have been here, and we saw it on the news. The beach and your amnesia. How terrible.' He's standing right in front of me now. Tall, with a rower's body, dark hair and blue-green eyes.

'I… Yeah.' God, what an idiot. I literally can't think of anything to say. At least he knows what happened, saving me having to explain everything.

His smile broadens. 'I'm Jack Harrington, club coach and fellow rower.' He holds out his hand and I shake it. 'I'm guessing you can't remember me?' he says.

'Sorry, no.'

He puts his hand on his heart, steps back and pretends to be offended.

'But if it's any consolation,' I say with a hesitant smile, 'I can't remember anyone, or anything, so it's not just you.'

'Okay, I'll let you off. Do you want a cuppa? I was just locking up, but we can go back upstairs and sit on the deck for a while if you like?'

'No, that's okay,' I say. 'Thanks for the offer but I'd better get back.' I don't know why I turned him down. A chat and a cuppa with a former-friend sounds like it could be just what I need, but I'm a little tired and off-balance.

'No worries,' he says. 'Another time, maybe?'

'Sure. That would be great,' I say. I make a move to leave, but then I turn back. 'Apparently I used to row here.'

'Only every day,' Jack says with a grin.

I have a thought. 'Maybe… Do you think I could book in a session some time? I might need help remembering what to do, though.'

'Of course. Give me a call, or better yet just drop by. I go out most mornings around 7 am.'

'Great. Thanks so much. I lost my mobile so I don't have anyone's numbers, but I'll definitely drop by one morning.'

'Look forward to it. Good to see you, Mia. Take care.'

'Bye.'

I walk away feeling more optimistic. He seemed like a nice guy. Easy to talk to. Hopefully, I'll remember how to row. Maybe it's like riding a bike – something you never forget. It seems like something I might really enjoy.

Maybe the old me is starting to resurface? Meeting old friends, getting back to my old hobbies, rediscovering my house, my town.

Maybe.

CHAPTER TEN

Sitting on the balcony with a tuna salad and a glass of dry white wine, I sigh with pleasure at having an evening to myself to relax. I gaze out over the river, at the boats going by – the sail boats, canoeists, pleasure boats, rowers. Funny to think that I'm actually one of them. That I used to spend so much of my time out on the water. Maybe I will again.

A loud ringing makes me jump. A phone. Must be the landline. Its shrillness sets my pulse racing. Who could it be? Piers? I want to ignore it and carry on sitting here with my thoughts. But what if it's important?

I swallow a mouthful of salad, but it's still lodged in my throat as I make my way inside towards the intrusive sound. I don't even know where I keep the phone, but I locate it quickly enough, on the breakfast bar.

'Hello?'

There's a pause, and then 'Mia, is that you?' A woman's voice, with an east-coast accent, maybe London or Essex.

'This is Mia,' I say.

'Are you okay? Cara saw a post about you on Facebook. Said you lost your memory. Is it true?'

'Sorry, who is this?' I ask.

Silence on the other end of the line. Whoever it is has tried to cover the mouthpiece and is talking to someone else. I make out the muffled words: 'She asked me who I am. Maybe it's true.'

'Hello?' I say.

'Sorry, I'm here,' she replies. 'Mia, don't you recognise my voice?'

'No,' I say. 'That post you saw on Facebook was right. I did lose my memory. Who is this?'

'Mia, it's me. It's your mum.'

I don't know what to think, what to feel. I don't recognise her voice and I can't picture her face.

'Mia, are you there? Mia?'

'I'm here,' I say, my voice only a fraction above a whisper.

'Can you remember who I am? Can you remember your sister?'

'I'm sorry,' I reply, 'but I don't remember anything or anyone. I don't remember you.' I feel a whooshing in my ears, my heart pumping hard. It's as though I'm hearing myself from a long way away.

'Oh my God, Mia. That's terrible. What happened to you, sweetheart? Are you okay? Are you hurt at all?'

I don't feel like I can have this conversation now. The thought of explaining everything that's happened makes me feel exhausted. 'I'm fine.'

'You don't sound fine. You sound... different. Let me come and see you. I can take time off work. Say it's a family emergency. It can't be easy, losing all your memories. You'll need someone with you. Someone to take care of you.'

I try to picture my mother here, looking after me, but the thought of another relative stranger in my house fills me with panic. 'Why don't I come to you instead? I could come tomorrow? Piers said you live in London.'

'What else did he say?'

'Nothing much. So, shall I? Come to you, I mean?'

'We-ll...' She doesn't sound too sure. 'Will you be able to get up here okay? After what you've just been through? I don't want you overdoing it.'

'I'll be fine.'

'Okay, if you're sure. I'll get Cara to take the day off, too.'

'Cara?'

'Your sister. God, you really have lost your memory. Don't worry, hon, we'll take care of you. Just jump on a train and get yourself home. You know, there are probably some trains still running tonight.'

'Tonight?' The thought of travelling to London tonight is too much. 'Not tonight,' I say. 'Tomorrow would be better.'

'Well, alright. But make it first thing. I'm worried about you, Mia, sweetheart. I need to see you and make sure you're okay.'

'Thanks,' I say, not quite able to call her "Mum" yet. She does sound really worried about me. Maybe when I see her and my sister I'll remember some of my past. I hope so.

'Cara was beside herself when she saw that post on Facebook. She thought it was some kind of hoax. Couldn't believe it could be true. How did it happen? It said you were found on the beach. You weren't attacked were you?'

'No, no. I'm fine, honestly.'

'How can you be fine when you've lost your memory?'

'Don't worry, I'll tell you all about it tomorrow. Can you give me your address?'

Her voice goes muffled again as she speaks to the person in the background, presumably my sister: 'She doesn't even know our address.' And then she comes back on the line and gives me her address, phone number and directions of how to get to her house in South West London.

When I finally end the call, my head is spinning. I'm not sure how to feel. I can't stop my brain whirring, trying to picture the woman behind the voice on the phone. What does she look like? Surely I must have a photo of her somewhere. I glance around the apartment, but I can see no photos on display at all, which strikes me as odd. Not even of me and Piers. I'll have to hunt some out. I must have family photos somewhere. I also realise I need to find out the train times.

The phone rings again, making me jump out of my skin. Maybe it's my mum calling me back. She must have forgotten to tell me something.

'Hello?'

'Is that Mia?' A woman, but it's not my mum. It's a younger voice. Vaguely familiar.

'Yes, this is Mia.'

'It's DS Emma Wright here, from CID.'

'Oh, yes, hi.' Nerves kick in. Why are the police calling me?

'How's your memory?' she asks. 'Any improvement?'

I pause, deciding how much to tell her. 'I actually did have one small memory,' I eventually reply. 'I had a dream about the rowing club. I just got an image of it, though. Nothing specific.' I leave out the detail of the woman, like I have with everyone else, wondering if in this instance I should tell her.

'Well that's good news,' she says. 'Hopefully, that's the start of you getting all your memories back.'

'Hope so.'

'I'm just ringing with a progress report,' she says. 'Nothing to worry about, but I have a bit of news for you.'

'Okay,' I reply, curious.

'We'd like you to know that unless any new evidence comes to light, we're treating your case as an accident, so you can rest a bit easier.'

'Oh, okay, an accident.' I repeat the words. To be honest, I didn't really consider the fact that it could be anything else. No one gave me any reason to believe otherwise. .

'Yes,' she continues. 'After investigation, it appears you went rowing very early on Sunday morning,' she says. 'A fishing vessel found your abandoned boat out in the Channel this morning. We think you must have capsized, hit your head and been swept out to sea which is how you ended up on Southbourne Beach.'

'Wow,' I say.

'Yes. Looks like you're one very lucky lady. You could easily have drowned out there.'

'Wow,' I say again, sinking down onto one of the kitchen stools.

'Are you okay?' she asks.

'Yes,' I reply. 'I'm fine. I guess it's just a relief to finally know what happened.'

'Of course.'

We chat for a few moments more. I tell her about my mum calling, and about my brain scan results, and she asks me to contact her if I remember anything else that could be important. But, apart from that, this feels like the end of it. Now, it's simply a case of me trying to regain my memories and get on with my life.

I hang up the phone, exhausted. The room feels suddenly darker, the evening turning to night. Through the open doors to the balcony, I see yellow and white lights winking on along the river. My supper is still out there on the table, but I no longer feel hungry. I think again about the police woman's words. I was swept out to sea. How frightened I must have been. No wonder I blocked it out. It really is a miracle that I survived at all. I realise my left leg is trembling, and my breathing is becoming heavier. I need to calm down. Maybe I'm in shock. I breathe in slowly through my nose, and out through my mouth. Deep steadying breaths. My fingers tingle and my head feels light, like there's nothing in it. I realise I'm about to pass out, so I purposely slide off the stool and sink to the floor. That way, I won't have far to fall...

CHAPTER ELEVEN

I open my eyes to find myself staring at the cream sofa back. I remember last night – passing out, then coming to on the kitchen floor. I managed to haul myself up and gulp down a glass of water before making it onto the sofa, curling up and falling asleep. Now, it's morning, and I turn over and blink at the brightness. My neck is cricked where I slept with my head pressed up against the arm of the sofa. Yesterday's memories wash over me like waves. My mum calling… DS Wright from CID telling me how I capsized in the sea… my lunch with Piers. Everything hits me, buffeting my brain with an overload of information. I close my eyes and turn over to face the back of the sofa again, wishing I could go back to sleep. To oblivion. It hurts to think.

But, I remember, I'm supposed to be going to London today. I could cancel, I suppose, but I really do want to meet my mother and sister. They appear to be the only family I've got. They could be the ones to help me get my memories back. I take a breath, open my eyes and sit up too quickly, feeling like I left my head on the sofa cushion. After a few seconds, I feel steadier, the room comes back into focus so I lurch shakily to my feet. I notice that I left the doors to the balcony open all night, and a coolish breeze has ensured the room isn't too stifling. My tuna salad and glass of Prosecco must still be out there, too, wilted and flat.

My dress is crumpled, my mouth tastes vile and I have a pounding headache. First things first, I need to find some paracetamol or aspirin, brush my teeth, have a shower then make myself some breakfast. After that, I'll tackle train times and the rest.

Two and a half hours later, I'm on the train, staring out of the window, the chair material hot and prickly beneath my thin cotton dress. Opposite me, two smartly dressed women chat excitedly about shopping and a theatre visit. The seat next to me is empty and I've placed my handbag on it, in an attempt to deter anyone from sitting there.

It's only a few minutes after ten, so I should be in London by lunchtime. My headache has cleared up and I'm suddenly infused with optimism. I'm not sure what happened to me last night. Perhaps a touch of exhaustion. I'm constantly having to process new information about my life, and I did do an awful lot yesterday.

Maybe meeting my mum will give me a sense of belonging. Anchor me. I wonder what my sister's like, what our relationship is like. Do we get on? Is she older or younger than me? Are we close? I hope so. I don't want to build up my hopes too much, in case I'm disappointed.

The train journey goes by quickly enough. I gaze at the fields and houses, the factories and warehouses, daydreaming about nothing in particular. I eavesdrop on the women sitting opposite whose superficial conversation soothes me. I feel included somehow, even though they pay me no attention. And then the relaxed atmosphere on the train changes as we pull into Waterloo Station and everyone busies themselves gathering belongings and dealing with the subtle etiquette of moving out from their seats, into the aisle and finally off the train onto the platform.

I manage to navigate the underground with ease – strangely, I discover I know how the system works. I know the names of the main tube stops, even though I don't recognise the name of the place my family lives – a suburb called Southfields. This underground network is familiar to me, its dull greys and browns, its warm, burnt musty scent, the hum of tube trains pulling away into dark tunnels, and the screech of brakes as they arrive. The throngs of people moving as one, downwards, upwards, along corridors and platforms. Purposeful. I move along with them, comfortably swept up in their colourful rush. Eventually, I reach my stop and emerge into bright sunshine once more.

Southfields isn't anything like I imagined. I thought it would be more built up, more urban, but it actually has quite a village-y feel. As I follow the directions my mum gave me, I find myself walking past designer boutiques, bistros, delicatessens and cafés. And, lovely though it is, none of it looks familiar. At the end of the High Street, I turn into a tree-lined residential street flanked with characterful Edwardian terraces. The sun dapples my face through the leaves. It's a pleasant walk and I almost forget why I'm here.

Not too far now. Just a couple of streets away and I'll be there. My stomach swoops with a sudden attack of nerves. Questions flit through my mind once more. What will my family be like? Will I like them? Will I recognise them? Or will it be like with Piers where I feel no connection? I want to belong. To be part of a family, rather than simply a person on the periphery of things. I suppose I'll find out soon enough.

I turn left, and then right, and finally, find myself in Smith-bridge Close. Straight ahead sits the block of flats where my mum lives. Is this the place where I grew up? It's a low, wide building, set out in a horseshoe shape. Built from yellow bricks, it has that ex-local authority look about it. I can't help feeling disappointed that they don't live in one of the pretty Edwardian terraces I just passed.

A group of kids on bikes and skateboards are hanging out in the car park, chatting and laughing. As I walk past, they pause to glance at me, but I'm obviously not interesting enough, as they turn straight back to their conversation.

The front door to the block is one of those heavy-duty wooden fire doors, its glass embedded with wire mesh. The buzzer for number 2B is easy to spot, near the top of the list. Written next to it in smudged blue biro is the name F. Richards. I wonder if that's my mum's name. I press the buzzer and wait.

Seconds later, there's a reply.

'That you, Mia?'

'Yes, it's me.'

'Come in. Turn right, off the hall.'

The door buzzes and I push it open, walking into a large, warm, dim hallway that smells of last night's dinner combined with peach-scented air freshener. I smooth down my dress, run my fingers through my hair and turn right, down a long corridor. Before I'm halfway down, the door at the end opens.

'Mia!' A woman stands in the doorway. She's short and slim with a greyish blonde bob. I walk a little faster. I guess this must be my mum. With a jolt of disappointment, I realise I don't recognise her. When I reach the doorway, she takes my hand and kisses my cheek. Her hand is cold, and she smells of perfume and cigarette smoke.

'Come in, sweetheart. Come in.'

I follow her through a narrow hallway hung with water-colour prints, past several doors until we reach the end where the lounge is situated. A girl sits on a faux leather sofa chewing a lock of hair. She's the spitting image of my mother, but her hair is longer and blonder. She stands when she sees me and gives a hesitant smile.

'Hi, Mia,' she says.

'You must be Cara,' I say.

She and my mum give each other a look. I don't blame them. It must be so strange for them – the fact that I don't know who they are.

'Yeah, I'm Cara,' she says. 'Can you really not remember us at all?'

I shake my head.

'Shit,' she says. 'That's mad.'

'You want a cuppa?' my mum asks. 'Tea? Coffee? Something stronger?' She laughs.

'Tea's good,' I reply.

'Cara?'

'Yeah, tea,' she replies.

My mum nods and leaves the room, and it feels a little uncomfortable with me and Cara just standing there. She's much shorter than me, even in her four-inch spike-heel sandals. I try to see if there's any resemblance at all between us. But all I see is a pretty young woman with dyed blonde hair and too much makeup. I feel wildly undergroomed by comparison. But I don't think I could ever carry off her look.

'So,' I say, desperate to break the awkward silence. 'Am I older or younger than you?'

'You're two years older,' she says, scratching her nose with a perfectly manicured leopard-print fingernail.

'So, that would make you…'

'Twenty-three,' we say at the same time, punctuated by a small laugh. She sits back down on the sofa, gesturing for me to do the same.

There's a set of open patio doors at the end of the room, leading out to a small terrace screened by a low hedge. Beyond that is the entrance carpark, and I can hear the voices of the youths I passed earlier.

'So,' Cara says, 'you, like, can't remember anything about us? Not growing up here, or school, or anything?'

'I can't even remember my own boyfriend,' I say. 'I couldn't remember what my face looked like. I looked in the mirror, and didn't recognise myself. That was scary.'

'That's mental. You've got to tell mum. She won't believe it. She already thinks it's some kind of wind up.'

'She can call the hospital if she doesn't believe me,' I say. Strangely, I notice myself modifying my accent a little as I talk to Cara, taking on more of a London twang. Is this how I normally talk? Or has being around Piers made me lose my accent?

My mum comes back into the room carrying a tray with three mugs and a plate of pink wafer biscuits. I take a mug gratefully and sip at the liquid. It's a hot day, but the tea is refreshing.

'Mia doesn't remember anything,' Cara says. 'Nothing at all. She didn't even know what she looked like in the mirror.'

'That's terrible,' my mum replies. She settles herself on the sofa next to me. 'Let me look at you, Mia.'

I put my tea down on the glass coffee table.

Cara laughs. 'She really has lost her memory.'

'Why did you say that?' I ask.

'You dared to put your tea down on the table without using a coaster. You obviously forgot what mum's like about stuff like that.'

My cheeks grow warm. I pick up the mug and place it on one of the black leather coasters. 'Sorry,' I murmur.

'Cara!' My mum glares at her. 'Don't mind her,' she says to me. 'She's just winding you up. I don't care where you put your mug, sweetheart. You could pour your tea all over the rug and I wouldn't give a hoot. I'm just happy to have you here, safe and well.'

Cara mumbles something, but I don't hear what.

The room falls silent. We sip our tea.

'So,' my mum says. 'You going to tell us what happened to you? How you lost your memory?'

'I'm not really sure how it happened,' I reply. 'After you called last night, I got a call from the police. They think it was a rowing accident. That I capsized and was swept out to sea, but then I washed up on the beach. They said I'm really lucky to be alive.'

'My God, Mia,' my mum says, taking my hand in hers and kissing it. 'You nearly died!'

'How come you were rowing?' Cara says. 'Were you, like, in a boat on your own?'

'Yeah. Apparently I like to row.'

'Weird,' Cara says.

'So, didn't I used to row? Growing up?'

'Er, no.'

'I didn't know it was something you were into, love,' my mum says. 'Sounds dangerous. Perhaps you shouldn't do it anymore.'

It strikes me as really odd that they don't know about a sport I apparently love. 'Are you sure I never mentioned it to you?' I say, rubbing at my temple. 'It's one of the things I love to do. Why wouldn't I have told you about it?'

'You probably did mention it, love,' my mum replies. 'You know what I'm like – brain like a sieve.'

Another silence cloaks the room. Cara picks at the hem of her denim cut-offs, and my mum helps herself to a biscuit while I rack my brains for conversation.

'I hope you don't mind me saying,' I say, 'but we don't look very similar.'

'That's cos you look like your dad,' my mum says.

'Oh, right. I don't suppose you have a photo?'

'Cara, can you get the album? It's in my room on the dresser.'

Cara puts her tea down on the tray and stares at my mum, giving her a look I can't decipher.

'The album, Cara,' my mum repeats. 'Or do I have to do everything myself?'

Cara peels herself reluctantly from the sofa and leaves the room.

'My dad died, right?' I ask my mum.

'Yes, I'm sorry. You and Cara have different dads. Me and your dad – Marcus – we split up when you were a baby. You never really knew each other, which is a shame. And then he died a few years back. I met Steven, Cara's dad, soon after Marcus left. Me and Steve got married. Stayed together for eighteen years, and he brought you up like his own. We're still friends, but he's with someone else now. He'll be shocked when I tell him what's happened to you.'

I try to take it all in, but it's like she's talking about someone else's life. Someone else's family. I can't relate to any of it. I don't feel any kind of emotion, other than a simmering panic that I'm in the wrong place with the wrong people.

Cara comes back into the room with a chunky looking photo album. She sits on the other side of my mum, so now we're all squashed onto the one sofa together.

'Right, let's have a look,' my mum says, taking the album from Cara and opening it at the beginning.

'I've just realised,' I say to her, 'I don't know your name.'

She turns to me and strokes my cheek. 'Oh, Mia. It breaks my heart. How can you not even remember your own mum's name? I'm Fiona. Fiona Richards.'

'Would you mind if I called you Fiona, rather than *Mum*. It's just… it feels too strange at the moment.'

'Of course,' she says. But then I see her wipe a stray tear from her cheek.

'Oh, no,' I say. 'Forget that. I'm sorry. That's an awful thing to ask, isn't it? Of course I'll call you Mum. I'm sure I'll get used to it again.'

'Whatever makes you most comfortable, sweetheart. It's not a problem.' She sniffs and then smiles as she gazes down at the album. I follow her gaze.

'Look at the state of you, Mum,' Cara says. 'You look well pissed in that photo.'

A younger version of my mother leans against a good looking man with dark hair, his arm around her waist. Her eyes are unfocused and she does look slightly drunk. But she also seems happy. Her clothes are casual – jeans and a vest top, her hair tumbling down around her shoulders in blonde waves. The man wears jeans and a white t-shirt. He's much taller than her, staring directly at the camera, as though he's looking at me. Seeing right into my soul.

'That's your dad, Marcus,' my mum says. Although I already guessed that much. 'Handsome devil wasn't he.'

'Yes,' I agree, my eyes glued to the photo. 'Yes, he was.'

My mum closes the album and passes it back to Cara. 'Put that back in my room, love.'

'Oh,' I say. 'Can't I see some more? Are there any of me and Cara growing up? Maybe they'll help me remember.'

'These are just pictures of me,' my mum says. 'Of my younger days. They'll be boring for you.'

'Do you have any of me?' I ask.

'Yes, of course, but they're—'

'They're in storage,' Cara interrupts.

'Yes,' my mum agrees. 'This place was getting cluttered, so I had a clear out. The albums are in storage, but I'll go and get them soon. Then you can come over again and take a look.'

My shoulders droop. I had hoped that seeing photos of my childhood would help me get my memory back. Never mind.

The rest of the day passes quickly and pleasantly enough. We talk some more about my childhood, about school and growing up. But I don't remember any of the things they tell me. Not a single thing.

As the day wears on, my mum becomes more and more emotional. She's worried about me, and begs me to stay for the whole weekend. But the thought fills me with dread. I find my sister a little intimidating. She's friendly enough, but I don't relish the idea of staying overnight. Even though, it turns out, this is the rented flat I grew up in, where she and I shared a room for over twenty years. No, I can't stay here. I crave the peace and solitude of my own house, so I leave my mum and sister at around five o'clock. My mum cries, and I feel bad for her. But not bad enough to stay.

The journey home is a nightmare, with commuters crammed into the train carriages, and no spare seats, so I have to stand for the entire ninety-minute journey back to Christchurch. I almost fall into a taxi at the station, and I'm too tired to think about anything other than the fact that I'm so pleased to be nearly home. My shoulders relax as we cruise down Christchurch High Street. The town is fairly quiet for a Friday evening, just a few clusters of people heading into the local pubs, wine bars and restaurants.

At last, we cross the stone bridge which leads to my house. I'm looking forward to washing the travel-grime off my skin and having something to eat. The taxi comes to a stop, its engine still running, and I pay the driver, adding on a generous five-pound tip. I step outside, breathing in the familiar river air, and fumble about in my bag for my house keys, panicking for a few seconds when I don't locate them instantly. I finally wrap my fingers around them, unlock the front door and stumble inside.

Home.

Something's wrong. I realise the alarm isn't bleeping. I'm sure I set it this morning. My body tenses. Should I be worried? Is someone here? An intruder? But my fear turns to annoyance as my brain catches up and I realise who it is.

'Mia! Is that you?' His voice floats down the stairs.

Shit, I'm right. It's Piers.

CHAPTER TWELVE

Dual feelings of relief and irritation flood my body. It's not an intruder. Piers must have let himself in with his spare set. I think I might have to get those keys back off him. I get the feeling it won't be easy.

'Hi, Piers!' I call up the stairs, my voice shaky. I could cry – I'm all talked out. I don't have the energy to tell him about my day. I just want to be on my own. Can I ask him to leave? No, probably not. I'm going to have to play the sweet girlfriend. It's not his fault I turned into someone else. I take a deep breath and begin to climb the staircase. His face appears, peering down at me from the top floor.

'Thank God you're back,' he says.

'Why? What's happened?' I jog up to the top and kiss him on the cheek. He pulls me into a hug and then pulls back, staring at my face intently.

'Are you okay?' he says. 'Where've you been? I've been going out of my mind with worry, Mia. You need to get yourself another phone so you can let me know where you are.'

'Why? What's the matter?'

'*What's the matter?*' he repeats. 'You just vanished. I came over this afternoon and you weren't here. No note. Nothing. You didn't call me to let me know where you were. Are you okay?'

'I'm fine,' I say, feeling a twinge of guilt. I guess I should have let him know where I was. He is supposed to be my boyfriend, and he doesn't have my new mobile number yet.

'Honestly,' he says, 'I was just about to call the police and all the hospitals. I had visions of you wandering around lost with no memory of anything. Where were you, anyway?'

'I'm sorry,' I say. 'I didn't know you'd be worried. I thought you'd be working.'

'You really do need to get a phone, Mia.'

'It's okay, I got one yesterday.'

'And you didn't think to give me the number? Or give me a call to let me know you were alright?' His worry is turning to anger. I'm trying to keep my temper under control, too. I'm not in the mood to deal with this right now.

'I need a shower,' I say. 'Give me ten minutes? And then we'll talk.'

'Do what you want, Mia. I'm going home.'

I've really pissed him off. My anger subsides. Even though I would rather he left, I realise I don't want him to go off in a mood. 'Hang on, Piers. Look, I'm sorry. I wasn't thinking straight. Please don't go. Don't be mad at me.' I realise that despite my irritation with Piers, I don't want to upset him. He genuinely seems to care about my wellbeing.

He scowls, but at least he makes no move to leave. 'I wanted us to spend the afternoon together,' he says. 'I made us a picnic.'

Now I really do feel like a bitch. He was trying to do something nice for me and I didn't spare him a second's thought. 'I'm so sorry,' I say. 'I mean it. I'm sorry. Look, come and sit down. Let's have a drink.' I take his hand and lead him over to the kitchen where he sits down on a bar stool and pulls me up close to him, his arms around my waist. I guess my quiet evening will have to wait while I try to make it up to him. 'How about I make us dinner this evening?' I say.

'Really?' He raises an eyebrow and looks doubtful.

'What's that look for? I'm sure I can rustle something up?'

'Cooking isn't really your strong point, babe,' he says with a reluctant smile.

'Cheeky.'

'Go ahead, then,' he says. 'I'm prepared to be proved wrong.'

'Let me just have a quick wash and get changed,' I say, 'and I'll be right back.' I try to disentangle myself from his embrace, but he pulls me back.

'You still haven't told me where you've been.'

'Pour me a glass of wine and I'll tell you all about it in a minute,' I reply.

He lets me go and I throw him a smile as I leave the room and head back downstairs to my room. It's sweltering in here, so I throw open the door to the balcony. Evening noises and aromas filter in. The sounds of someone cooking – pots and pans clanking, taps turning on and off, someone somewhere playing a Motown track. I strip off my clothes, dump them in the linen basket and walk into the en suite. Then, I step into the shower, turn on the spray and let the London grime slide down the plughole.

I'm hoping the cool water will energise me for the night ahead. At least Piers is here for me. I should give him a fair chance and shake off any negative thoughts I might have had about him. I owe him that much. I step out of the shower, pull on a bath robe and towel dry my hair, discarding both on the floor a minute later. My body is still a little damp, but the air is so warm that I'm guessing my skin will be dry by the time I'm back upstairs. Without too much thought, I pick out some fresh underwear, and another summery dress which I slip over my head. I don't bother with shoes or makeup.

I pad up the stairs, back to the living room, looking forward to my glass of wine. I glance around, but Piers doesn't appear to be up here any longer.

'Out here, babe!'

I cross the room and step out onto the balcony where he's sitting sipping a glass of red wine. He's wearing beige shorts, a pale blue short-sleeved shirt and aviator shades, his legs stretched out on the low coffee table next to a bowl of olives and a half-empty wine bottle. He hands me a glass and I sink into one of the armchairs.

'Cheers,' Piers says. We clink glasses and I take a healthy swig, relishing the warm alcoholic burn in my throat, and letting my shoulders relax. The sun is sinking, but the air still holds the heat of the day.

'So,' Piers says. 'Are you going to tell me where you've been all day?'

'I went to London,' I say. 'I went to visit my mum.'

'You did what?' He takes his feet off the table and sits bolt upright.

'She called me last night, worried out of her mind. I had to go and see her and Cara. Let them know I was okay.'

'Cara? You saw Cara?' Piers' face has turned a deep shade of red. He puts his glass down and removes his shades, leaning in towards me. 'Have you gone mad, Mia?'

'What? What's wrong with that?'

'I'll tell you what's wrong with that. Your sister is a money-grabbing little bitch and you haven't seen or spoken to her for three years.'

'And you didn't think to mention this to me *before*?' I hiss. His words set my whole body trembling. My sister – a money-grabber? We haven't spoken for three years? Is Piers telling the truth? I take another gulp of wine and put my glass on the table with shaking fingers.

'Well… I…' he stutters.

'Well?' I demand.

'I didn't think you'd go rushing off there without telling me,' he says throwing his hands up in the air. 'I'm sorry,' he adds. 'I should've—'

'Three years!' I interrupt him, still unable to believe what I'm hearing. 'I haven't spoken to Cara for three years? And what about my mum?'

'You haven't spoken to her either. She sided with your sister, so you cut them out of your life. Shit, Mia. I was going to tell you about them, but I didn't want to overload you with drama. Not after everything you've just been through. How the hell did you end up going to see them today?'

'I told you, my mum rang last night. Apparently Cara saw something online about me losing my memory.'

'Yeah, I bet she loved that. You losing your memory is the perfect opportunity to get back in your good books and hit you up for more cash.'

I suddenly feel cold. Sick. Could they really only have wanted to see me because I have money?

'Piers, there's something I still don't understand – how come I have money in the first place? I thought you said I was a teacher, but here I am, living in this house and driving a brand new car. Am I rich?'

Piers exhales and leans back into the sofa. He runs his hands over the top of his head. 'Yeah, Mia. You're rich. You don't need to work, and from everything you've told me, your sister is jealous as fuck.'

'So, how did I get my money? Did I win the lottery or something?'

'I don't know how much your mum told you, Mia,' Piers says. 'Did you know you and Cara have different fathers?'

'Yeah, she told me my dad's name was Marcus James, but he died three years ago. She showed me a photo.' In my mind, I see the image of that handsome man gazing out of the photograph at me. My father. A man I will never know.

'Yes, well, back when he knew your mum, Marcus was dirt poor. But later on in life he made a fortune out of some dodgy South American tree-planting scheme. I don't know the details. All I know is that when he died, he had no heirs other than you. You got everything.'

'How much?'

'Just over eight million.'

'Oh my God,' I say, my voice barely a whisper.

I sit there letting that information sink in.

I'm rich.

Really rich.

'Mia. Are you okay? I know it's a lot to take in.'

'So why did me and Cara fall out? Surely, I would have given mum and Cara some of the inheritance, wouldn't I? I can't spend eight million all by myself.'

'Yes, you gave them some, but they wanted more. You never really had a great relationship with them. You always said your mum preferred Cara. That they were a happy little unit – Cara and her mum and dad. You said you always felt like an outsider. That it was only when you inherited the money they started being nicer to you.

'Your mum said she was owed some of your inheritance because your dad never paid any maintenance while you were growing up. You were pissed off to hear your mum talking like that. That's how you ended up here, in Dorset. You got on a train and left London.'

'So I came here to get away from them. I thought I must have left London to be with you.'

'We only met last year, babe.'

Somehow, I assumed Piers and I had been together longer.

'So exactly how much of my inheritance did I give to my mum and sister?'

'I don't know. You don't like to talk about it. About them. You always said that they weren't part of your life anymore. That they were in your past.'

I think about what Piers has told me. I obviously didn't give either of them enough money to buy their own place. My mum's still renting and Cara lives with her. I must be really mad at them not to have at least bought them a place. With eight million pounds, I could easily afford it. I wish I could remember what they'd said or done to make me cut them out of my life.

'Mia?'

I realise Piers is talking to me. 'Sorry, what did you say?'

'I asked if you were okay.'

'Just trying to take it all in.' I pick up my glass and drain the contents.

'You should eat something,' he says.

'I'm not hungry. But I'll have another glass of wine.' I grasp the bottle, my hand shaking badly. Piers takes it from me and refills both our glasses.

'I think you're in shock,' he says. 'I still can't believe you went to see them today.'

I stare across at his tanned face, his features marred by a dark scowl.

My brain is whirling. Images of today's visit crowd my mind – my mum in tears, my dad's photo, Cara's leopard-print fingernails. Could they really be the money-grabbing people he says they are? I knock back another half-glass of wine and realise I'm drunk.

Placing my glass back down on the table, I get to my feet and pad over to the balcony's edge, holding onto the railing with both hands, staring out across the tranquil river. I feel the urge to laugh, or scream, or… something. Piers comes to join me.

'You okay, babe?'

I shrug. He puts an arm around my shoulder and kisses the side of my head. I turn and tilt my face up to his. Putting a hand to his cheek. Then, I let Piers kiss me. A soft, sweet, wine-flavoured kiss. Nothing too heavy. But I know it's not enough. I need something more to block out the confusion in my head. So I kiss him again. Harder.

My nerve endings tingle. It feels good to give into this. To know that I can hand myself over to him. To switch my brain off and think about nothing more than his mouth on mine, his hands sliding down my body.

'Jesus, Mia, you smell so good.'

We move into the lounge where he lifts my dress over my head. Moves his mouth down to my neck, my breasts. Somewhere, deep in my mind, I know I'm going to regret this. But for now... I don't care.

CHAPTER THIRTEEN

I made a mistake. A terrible mistake. What was I thinking?

Piers is asleep next to me, sprawled out across two-thirds of my bed, one arm flung across my waist. We slept together last night and – I'll admit it – it was good. I enjoyed it. A lot. But it was still a mistake. I don't know him properly. I don't know if we're right together. And now I've sullied the waters. Now he's going to think everything is back to how it was. And it isn't. Not by a long way.

Morning light floods the room, the curtains undrawn. A glance at the clock shows me it's only 6.25 am. I gently nudge Piers' arm off my body, tensing as he stirs and murmurs something unintelligible in his sleep. I'm not ready for him to wake up yet. I need a few moments more to collect my thoughts. He shifts onto his other side and settles back down. I let out a breath.

I think about everything he told me last night. About my family. I wish I knew how my mother really feels about me. She was certainly emotional yesterday. Maybe she regrets what happened in the past. But how can I know for sure? How can I find out? What reason would Piers have to lie about it?

An idea comes to me. I slip carefully out of bed, so as not wake Piers, and hook a short robe off the back of my bedroom door, sliding my arms into the cool cotton and tying the sash. Then, I tiptoe out of the room and down the two flights of stairs to the office on the ground floor. I haven't even been in this room yet. Not since the accident. But I hope I can find what I'm looking for.

I push open the door. It's a simple, square, white room with an oak floor. To my right, the wall is lined with bookcases. To my left sits a long, white desk and two grey office chairs. Straight ahead, wood-framed bifold doors lead out onto a pretty walled courtyard which currently sits in shade – the sun not yet high enough to reach this tiny north-facing garden.

I cast my eyes over the room once more. A laptop sits on the desk, plugged into the mains. I head over to it, perch myself on the edge of one of the chairs and flip open the lid, watching the machine hum into life. The screensaver is a photograph of me on the river. I'm rowing. My hair is scraped back into a ponytail, the sunlight illuminating my face. I briefly wonder who took the picture. Then, I click the email icon and the photo disappears, replaced by my inbox.

There's a list of around a dozen unopened emails, all of which appear to be special offers and spammy-type mails from various companies. Nothing personal at all. And, even stranger, there are no emails dated from before my accident. The earliest email was sent on Monday. Could someone have deleted them? Piers?

I check the Sent folder and the Trash folder, but there's nothing in them either. Maybe I have another email account? I go back to the desktop page, but there are no other email icons. Strange. I shift back in my seat and think for a moment.

A silver two-drawer filing cabinet sits under the desk to my left. I reach down, slide open the top drawer and scan the hanging files, my fingers hovering over them. It seems I'm quite an orderly person. Everything is clearly labelled in alphabetical order. I lift out a file entitled *Bank Account (Current)* and lay it open on the desk. There, meticulously filed in chronological order, are my bank statements.

Piers was right. I'm loaded. It's quite something to see that many zeros sitting in an account with my name printed across the top. He said I inherited the money three years ago. I wish I'd thought to ask him exactly when I'd received it. Never mind, it won't take me long to check.

I flip back through several statements and see that three-and-a-half years ago my bank account was overdrawn. It went into credit in April of that year when I received a tax rebate for £643.29. I stayed in credit for precisely two days, and then it went back into the red.

My finances were in the same sorry state right up until June of that year. And then – bingo. I received a deposit on June 25th for the amount of £8,430,560.02. No more going overdrawn for me. What must I have thought when I heard the news? Was I sad about my dad dying? Or excited about the money?

I check through my subsequent bank transactions. I was spending an obscene amount of money on clothing, jewellery and shoes. Then, at the end of July, I transferred two lump sums – one to my mum and one to my sister. Fifty grand each.

Fifty grand is a hell of a lot of money. But, considering I'd recently inherited eight million, it seems insulting to have given my family so little. Piers must be right – they must have behaved badly towards me. I can see no other reason why I would have been so mean. I scroll forwards again. I gave Cara another £50k in September. Then, in the same month, I transferred just under twenty grand to a car dealership. In October, I transferred out just over seven hundred thousand pounds to a solicitor. I'm guessing that must have been for my house. I jot down the name of the solicitor on a pad on my desk.

I look through the next two years' transactions where my spending appears to be a little less extravagant, apart from a few meals out and several eye-wateringly expensive holidays. Until, I come to this March, where I paid £25,000 to a business called JB Properties, followed by another payment of £345,000 to the same account.

Who is JB Properties? And what did I spend all that money on? I think I can probably guess.

'What are you doing down here?'

Piers' voice makes me jump out of my skin. I close the file, then I turn towards him with an overly bright smile that I instantly tone down a notch.

'It's not even seven o'clock yet,' he says with a yawn. He's wearing nothing but boxers, and his hair's dishevelled. He walks over to me, bends down, brushes my hair back with his hand and kisses my neck. I let him kiss me on the mouth before pulling away. I can't make the same mistake as I did last night. I have to stop this before it goes any further.

'What's JB Properties?' I ask.

He straightens up and narrows his eyes. 'It's a bit early for work isn't it? Why don't you come back to bed? I'll make you breakfast.'

'I can't go back to bed now. I'm too awake.'

'Breakfast then,' he says.

'Yeah, okay. But you still haven't answered my question.'

'JB is our company,' Piers says.

'We have a company?'

'Yes. I told you about it already.'

'I know I lost my memory before the accident, but I think I'd remember if you told me we owned a company together.'

Piers sits on the other chair and runs his fingers through his hair. 'God, Mia, it's too early to be talking business. Can I at least get a cup of coffee?'

'Good idea,' I say. 'Let's go upstairs and have a cuppa, and you can tell me all about our business.'

'Fine.' He stands and leads the way back upstairs.

I wonder why he never mentioned the company before now.

Once upstairs, he busies himself making coffee, while I boil the kettle for a cup of herbal tea. We don't speak until we have our mugs in hand and I lead the way over to the sofas. I curl up on the corner of one, tucking my legs beneath me. Piers sits opposite, looking defensive.

'You know, Mia, I don't like the way you just spoke to me down there. Like you were accusing me of something. Just to be clear, I haven't done anything wrong.'

'Sorry if it came out like that,' I say. 'I was just surprised, that's all. I saw this big chunk of money paid out to JB Properties and I wondered what it was all about.'

'That money was for a flat. We bought a flat in Southbourne.' He takes a sip of his coffee. 'I told you about the property developing business.'

'You told me you were a property developer, Piers. But you never said we'd bought a flat together.'

'It was actually your idea,' he says. 'You decided you wanted to invest your inheritance in property. We both thought it would be a good idea to tart up a few run-down sea-front apartments and rent them out or sell them on. The Southbourne flat is the first one we've bought. I've got my eye on a few others.'

'That does sound like a good idea,' I say. 'I just wondered why you never mentioned it before.'

'I didn't want to overload you, babe. You've been through a lot. Thought it was better to tell you everything gradually.'

'Okay.' I suppose that makes sense. 'So, we own the company jointly. Does that mean you put half the money in?'

He flushes. 'No. You put the money up. I put the hard work in. That's the deal.'

That doesn't sound like a very good deal to me, I muse. 'And what's my role in it?'

'Role?'

'What do I do? It's half my company, so I must do something. Day-to-day stuff?'

'No. I do all the work, I told you, babe. You just relax and take it easy. There's no need for you to get your hands dirty.'

All this new information is making my head whirl. It sounds a little shady to me. But I guess if I was in love with the guy, why shouldn't we have gone into business together? Some couples do that, don't they? They live together, work together.

'We'll have to go over everything again,' I say. 'I want to see the contract and how it all works.'

'Of course,' Piers says. 'You'll see it's all legit. And it all makes good business sense.'

I give Piers a weak smile. I'm not so sure about that. Not with me putting up all the money. And, now, all this is making me question what he told me about my family yesterday. I'll have to go and visit them again. I want them to be on my side. To love me. To want what's best for me, and not be drawn by the money. And if there is bad blood between us, maybe we can start again. We can fix it. I don't need all my millions. Maybe I can buy them a house…

I suddenly feel panicky again. Panicky and helpless. Trapped. Constantly reliant on other people to let me know what's been going on. I sip my tea, keeping my eyes down. I could kick myself for sleeping with Piers last night. What was I thinking? I wasn't. I drank too much wine too quickly and it went to my head. I'm such an idiot. And yet, I should be happy shouldn't I? Here I am in this picture postcard town, in my beautiful house with my gorgeous boyfriend and a ton of money, living this seemingly great life. But it doesn't feel like it's *my* life. I feel like an impostor.

The rock is grey and smooth with a flat top, the perfect size and shape for sitting on. Bright green moss clings to one side and dark water stains its base. In fact, now that I look closer, there's water beginning to pool around the rock, lapping at its sides. A dank chill seeps into my legs and I'm surprised to see that my shoes are wet. Thick, gloopy water spills rapidly over my feet and, before I even have time to draw breath, it's already up to my calves. The rock before me is suddenly half-submerged. Then I see with a twist of dread that the rising water is a strange shade of dark crimson. And I realise with ice-cold clarity that it's not water at all…

CHAPTER FOURTEEN

As I press the buzzer, I think about how weird it feels to be back at my mum's place so soon. When I left here yesterday, I thought it would be ages before I returned. My mum sounded pleased to hear from me when I called her earlier. Told me that of course I could come. That I was welcome anytime and I didn't have to call ahead. She said she'd give me a key. That it was my home, too. I wonder if I've ever invited her to visit me in Christchurch. Somehow I doubt it.

Piers and I have been on rocky ground since I quizzed him over our business partnership this morning. I could tell he was having a hard time trying to keep his cool. Then, once I'd finished asking him about everything, he tried to kiss me again. To get me back into bed. It's my own stupid fault for encouraging him in the first place. I fobbed him off by saying I needed to come back to London today. I probably shouldn't have told him my plans, but the words just slipped out.

I told him I needed to get things sorted out. That I needed to find out exactly what had gone on between me, my mum and my sister. Piers said he was only looking out for me, that I didn't remember just how much I hated them. That coming back to London would upset me. That it would be a terrible mistake.

Now I'm here, I'm starting to think maybe he's right. My nerves have started up – a herd of elephant-sized butterflies are stampeding around in my stomach. Added to that, it's the most uncomfortably sticky day. The hottest yet. The London air is thick and heavy – like breathing in treacle. At least back in Christchurch there's a breeze off the river. I debate whether or not I should just turn around, get back on the train and go home again. I'm not sure if I have the mental energy for this encounter.

No. I strengthen my resolve, I don't care how nervous I am, or how hot it is. I know I have to confront my mother and Cara. I have to know for sure. See if they'll confirm what Piers told me. It's not a conversation that should take place over the phone.

'That you, Mia?' My mum's voice comes over the intercom.

'Hi, yes, it's me.'

The door buzzes and I make my way inside and down the corridor. My mum's there in the doorway, like last time.

'Hi, love!' she calls. She pulls me into a hug which I awkwardly return. 'Come on in then. It's lovely to have you back so soon.'

Cara is stretched out on the sofa, dressed minimally in cotton shorts and a bikini top. 'Can't keep away, can you.' She looks up and grins.

'Hi, Cara.'

'Do you want tea?' my mum asks.

'Water would be good.'

'Glad you said that,' my mum replies. 'Even I can't drink tea today. It's baking. The thought of boiling the kettle…'

'Yeah, the train was terrible,' I reply. 'Sweltering.'

'Cara? You want some water, love?'

'No, I'll have a can of Coke.'

My mum nods and goes into the kitchen. Now that I'm here, it all seems so surreal. I want there to be a reasonable explanation for Piers' revelation. I want it all to have been a stupid misunderstanding. My mum comes back with the drinks and sits down, shoving Cara along a bit. Cara tuts, takes her Coke and sits up, crossing her legs. She opens the can and takes several deep gulps. I take a seat opposite them on the other sofa.

'It's so good to see you again, Mia,' my mum says, taking a tiny sip of her water and putting her glass down on a coaster. 'Do you want to do anything special today? We could go into town if you like? See some sights, do a bit of shopping. What do you think?'

'Yeah, maybe,' I reply. I may as well launch right into it. No point sidestepping the issue. 'But the reason I've come… I really wanted to talk to you both.'

'Oh, okay,' my mum replies.

They glance at each other and then back at me.

'What was it you wanted to talk about, sweetheart? Do you want to hear some more stories about when you were a little girl?'

'That would be nice. Maybe later. No, I really wanted to ask you something.'

'Go on,' my mum says.

Cara drains her drink and puts the empty can on the floor. I feel her eyes boring into mine, but I'm focusing on my mum. It's somehow easier to look at her than at Cara.

'Before Friday,' I say. 'When was the last time we saw each other?'

My mum's expression changes from one of expectant interest to something else I can't define. It's a look of sadness, anger and… embarrassment. I risk a glance at Cara. She has a look of sarcastic indignation, one eyebrow raised, her mouth curled into a mocking sneer.

'Well,' Cara says. 'You probably already know the answer to that, don't you? Seeing as how you asked the question in the first place.' Her voice is tight and accusing.

I've opened the can of worms, so I'd better deal with it. 'I haven't come here for an argument,' I say. 'I just want to know what happened between us. How we fell out so badly.'

'I'll tell you what happened,' my sister says bluntly. 'You were a bitch.'

'Cara!' my mum says, slapping my sister gently on the leg. 'Mia says she doesn't want an argument.'

'So,' I continue, refusing to be drawn, 'is it true that before this week we hadn't seen each other for three years?'

'Yes,' my mum replies. 'It's true. Oh, Mia, it's been horrible.' Tears begin to drip down her cheeks.

'Now look what you've done,' Cara says to me with a twist of her lip. 'Every time you show your face, you make mum cry.' She puts her arm around our mother's shoulders.

'I'm sorry,' I say. 'I just want to understand what's happened between us.'

'What's happened,' Cara says, 'is that you inherited a shitload of money from your dad, and then you pissed off out of London without even saying goodbye. You just left us a crappy little note.'

'Cara, that's enough,' my mum says, sniffing loudly. 'We all did and said things we shouldn't have. It was a tense time. But maybe now we can move on. Make up. We *are* family after all.'

'Pity she didn't remember that at the time,' Cara mutters.

'What is your problem?' I say. 'I'm here because I lost my memory. I have total amnesia. I'm trying to find out what happened between us. That person you're talking about – the old me – I don't even know that person. This is who I am now, so your bitching and whining means nothing to me. Okay?' My voice is harsh, almost aggressive. I haven't a clue where that outburst came from. My heart is hammering. I'm not at all prepared for this confrontation.

Cara's hostility radiates from every pore of her body. I can feel its bite. She sticks out her lower jaw and folds her arms across her chest.

'Why did I leave London?' I ask. 'What happened to make us fall out? Was it to do with the money?'

'For a start, your precious dad didn't help mum out at all,' Cara says.

'What, you mean financially?' I ask.

'Yeah. Financially, physically, morally. Nothing. He just left her, skint with a baby – *you*. And then, years later, we found out he was loaded. And he didn't leave anything to mum in his Will. He left it all to you. And you didn't give mum anything.'

'That's not exactly true,' I say. 'I gave her fifty thousand pounds. And I gave you double that.'

'You had another fifty thousand, Cara?' My mum looks up sharply at her.

Cara flushes.

'Cara?' my mum says.

'Mia agreed to pay off my debts if I promised to leave her alone.'

'Leave me alone?' This is becoming more complicated by the second. And I still don't know if I can trust anything coming out of either of their mouths. It even looks like they were keeping things from each other. I wish more than anything that my memory would choose to return now. I'm at such a disadvantage, not knowing what I did or said, how I behaved in the past, who I trusted, and who was using me.

'You said you'd give me another fifty thousand if I stopped contacting you,' Cara explains. 'You even made me sign an agreement.' She shakes her head and rolls her eyes.

'Why would I do that?' I demand. 'Why wouldn't I want you to contact me?'

Cara doesn't answer. Her lips are pursed. I look at my mum, but she's looking expectantly at Cara, too.

'Cara?' she says.

'What?'

'Why didn't I know about this extra money?' my mum asks her.

Cara doesn't reply.

Suddenly, I'm fed up with the whole situation. It seems ridiculous to be arguing about stuff that I can't even remember.

'Look,' I say. 'I don't know about you, but I'm willing to forgive and forget the past if you are. Maybe we can—'

'Oh, well that's just super of you,' Cara says in a mocking tone, cutting me off. 'Miss Moneybags is willing to forgive us poor peasants. Thank you, Your Highness. How kind.'

'For goodness' sake, Cara,' my mum says, rising to her feet. 'Just stop running your mouth off for once in your life. I can't hear myself think!'

Silence descends on the room. I wish I'd never come. This hasn't achieved anything other than to make me feel sick and depressed. It seems Piers was right. My sister is a cow.

'Okay, Cara,' I say, 'I can see you don't want to put this behind us or be "friends" or whatever, so why don't you go ahead and answer my question.'

'What question?' she sneers. 'You've asked so many since you waltzed back in here.'

'Why did I give you an extra fifty thousand pounds to leave me alone? Why would I need you to leave me alone?'

She doesn't reply.

'Are you going to answer your sister?'

'Why are you both ganging up on me?' she whines. 'She's the one who left with all her money.'

'I'd just like to know what you did to make me want to cut off all contact with you,' I say. 'Is that an unreasonable question?'

'Fine.' She uncrosses her arms and pushes her hair back off her face. Suddenly she looks nervous… and a lot younger. 'I'll tell you. But you blew it up out of all proportion. It's not as bad as it sounds.'

'Cara, spit it out.' My mum's face is hard, her eyes hooded, her lips pressed in a firm line.

'Okay, fine,' she says, re-crossing her arms. 'But you won't like it.'

CHAPTER FIFTEEN

I can't imagine what my own sister could possibly have done that was so bad I had to pay her to leave me alone. I almost don't want to know.

'Well,' Cara says. 'For a laugh, I took a video on my phone of Mia and her ex having sex.'

'You did what!' my mum cries.

'It was just a laugh. I told her I'd put it online if she didn't help me out. But I would never actually have—'

'Cara Richards!' My mum rises to her feet. 'I am ashamed! She's your sister for crying out loud!'

'Half-sister,' she mutters.

'You were blackmailing me?' I shake my head and stare at her, open-mouthed. Of all the things I expected to hear, this wasn't one of them. 'You're telling me that you were going to post sex tapes of me online if I didn't give you more money?' My stomach churns. How could she do that? Firstly, that she would video me… and secondly, that she would use it to get money.

'You're making it sound worse than it was,' Cara says.

'How can I make it sound worse? Blackmail is blackmail, isn't it?'

'There's no point me trying to explain it,' Cara says. 'You'll just twist it like you always do.'

'Twist it? It sounds horrific enough without any "twists".'

My mum's face has gone white. It's obvious she knew nothing about this.

'Surely you didn't need to resort to blackmail?' I say. 'I would've given you the money if you needed it. You're my sister.'

'Yeah, you'd think that would count for something, wouldn't you,' she says.

'Where's the video now?' I ask.

'You deleted it.'

'How do I know you're telling the truth?'

'You don't… But I am.'

'Great,' I say. 'I can see that Piers was right. I really shouldn't have come back.'

'You weren't going to give us anything, Mia,' Cara says. 'Nothing at all. I had to beg you for the pittance you did give us. And what about Mum? She—'

'Don't bring me into it, Cara,' my mum says. 'I'm disgusted with your behaviour. I don't even want to look at you.' She turns to me, 'I'm sorry, Mia, but I think it's probably best if you leave.'

I stare back at her. 'Oh,' is all I can say. I stand up, feeling a little unsteady.

'It's nice that you came, but I think tempers are running a little high around here. Maybe we should have a break and meet again when we've had a chance to let the dust settle. Okay?' It's not a question she requires an answer to.

'Fine,' I say. 'I was just trying to—'

'I know.' She cuts me off. 'But now it's time for you to leave. In fact…' she turns to Cara, 'you can get out, too.'

'What!'

'Yes. I'm actually sick of the pair of you. Out! Leave me in peace.' Her voice has become loud and quavery.

'This is your fault.' Cara shoots me a venomous look. 'And if you want to know why there aren't any photos of you here, it's not because they're "in storage" – she mimes air quotes – 'It's because, after you left three years ago, I ripped them up and threw them in the bin with all the other rubbish. I didn't want your smug face staring at me. I didn't want you as a sister anymore. I still don't. You might have lost your memory, but you still think you're better than us.'

'That's enough, young lady,' my mum snaps at her.

I'm stunned by the depth of Cara's hatred for me. That she would destroy all my childhood photos seems worse than anything else she might have done. I quickly turn to go, loath to leave the house at the same time as my sister.

'Sorry you have to go, love,' my mum says, reaching out to touch my arm. 'But it's brought all the nastiness rushing back, and I can't cope with it. My nerves won't take it.'

'I'm sorry,' I say. 'I didn't mean for it to—'

'I know you didn't,' she says. 'But that's how it is. We'll talk again soon, when I'm feeling up to it.'

'Okay,' I say, guilt plucking at me. I didn't think I'd personally said anything that awful, but Cara had behaved like I was the devil. I'd almost expected her to physically attack me, she was so angry and bitter. I don't know how today has spiralled so out of control.

I leave the flat in a rush. Dazed, I head back to the tube with my pulse still racing. What the hell was all that about? I went there to get answers, hoping for a reconciliation. Instead, I feel more alone than ever. My goal of getting my memory back seems to be receding. I had hoped that spending time with my family would make me remember who I am. Instead, it's thrown up more questions. Questions I'm not sure I want the answers to.

The train journey home is a blur. Today has been way more than I ever bargained for. The words *blackmail* and *sex tapes* are lodged in my brain – ludicrous words that shouldn't be anything to do with me. Is my sister for real? Any hopes of us reconnecting have been well and truly severed.

I step out of the taxi and slot my key into my front door. I'm home. Safe. I make a resolution to leave the past alone. If my memory doesn't return, I'll start my life from scratch again. No family. No Piers. Just me, and whatever life I can create for myself. I'm rich. I have the luxury of doing what I want. I do like it here in Christchurch, but maybe I should go away somewhere where nobody knows me.

Dance music filters down from somebody's balcony. The sound of laughter – someone else's Saturday evening. As I open my front door, the music gets louder. It's coming from… upstairs. It's really loud. Thumping. Piers is here again! The mood I'm in, I feel like marching up the stairs and telling him to get lost. I don't care if he is my boyfriend. This is my house and he can't keep letting himself in anytime he feels like it. It's like I'm under attack from all sides. I want to scream. Instead, I slam the door behind me and stomp up the stairs, anger pulsing inside my head, growing, pounding, prickling at my skin.

'She's here!' a woman's voice cries out above the music.

What the hell?

A pair of feet appears on the stairs, walking down towards me. Denim-clad legs, a white shirt. It's Piers. His eyes are bright. He's smiling, holding a bottle of beer.

'What's going on?' I hiss. 'Are there people here?'

'I know you've had a crap time recently,' he says, kissing me with beer breath, draping his arms around my body. 'And I know today's visit will have been shit, so I rang round a few of our friends and invited them over. Thought it would cheer you up. It's Saturday night, babe. And I know how much you love to party.'

If I'd thought today couldn't get any worse, Piers just proved me wrong.

'Who knows,' he adds, his voice slurred with drink. 'Maybe you'll recognise someone and your memory will come back. What can I get you to drink? Wine? Vodka tonic?' He doesn't notice my glare, or if he does, he chooses to ignore it.

I'm suddenly defeated by his cheerful onslaught. I feel my shoulders slump. 'Yeah,' I say. 'Vodka tonic sounds good.'

All my anger evaporates. Piers has filled my house with friends who may as well be complete strangers randomly picked up off the street, because I know I'm not going to recognise a single one of them. Could my boyfriend possibly be the most insensitive man on the planet? Short of storming upstairs and yelling at everybody to get the hell out, I have no choice but to make the best of this. The only choice now, the only way for me to get through this farcical evening, is to get spectacularly wasted.

'Make it a large one,' I say.

'That's my girl,' he says with a grin.

I run my fingers through my hair, push my shoulders back and follow him up the stairs, wondering what new hell I'm about to encounter.

'Mia!'

'Oh my God, Mia, we heard what happened.'

'How are you?'

'Piers told us what happened. We can't believe it.'

'Mia!'

'Hey, Mia.'

As the music throbs, pulsing through my core, my house swarms with beautiful people, all crowding around me, kissing me on the cheeks, hugging, offering condolences and well wishes. The women with their shiny hair, bright designer dresses, perfume, lip gloss and sparkling jewellery. The men confident and tanned in shirts and shorts, their aftershave subtle but expensive. Everyone's giving me the same weird, fascinated smiles and pitying looks, like I'm some strange museum exhibit. I bet they've all been gossiping about me. Loving the drama.

I smile back and nod, saying I'm fine, knocking back the vodkas, letting all the people merge into one big smiling face of concern. Piers steers me from one to another, introducing them, telling me how I came to know each person. I don't even attempt to take in the information. I simply nod and smile politely, gulping at my drink, waiting until the blissful moment I can pass out and forget this hellish day.

I pretend I'm happy to see them all. I laugh at their jokes, kiss Piers, hang off his arm, make a good show of enjoying his concerned attention. But inside I'm fuming. He says this will help me get back to normal. That maybe I'll recognise someone. But I don't. Of course I don't. If I can't even recognise my own mother, how would I recognise a bunch of strangers? Inside I'm laughing hysterically. Laughing and screaming.

'This is Suki and Matt Willis,' Piers says. 'From next door.'

My heart skips a beat as I realise I recognise them. But disappointment hits me when I realise I don't remember them from before the accident – it's the couple I saw arguing in the driveway the other morning when I was having breakfast on the balcony. They look a little older than me and Piers, maybe in their mid-thirties. They don't fit in well with the rest of the crowd here tonight. They're older and more conservatively dressed. Matt is short and broad, he's almost square, half a head shorter than his wife. But he has an open, friendly face with grey-flecked short, brown hair. Suki is an English-rose with a dark brown bob, dressed in an expensive-looking, knee-length fitted dress. She doesn't smile or acknowledge me in any way. She just looks bored.

I nod and smile at them, my eyes becoming heavy as the vodka does its work.

'Hello, Mia,' Matt says warmly. 'Sorry to hear about what happened. If there's anything Suki and I can do to help, you will let us know, won't you. We're just next door, and Suki's home most days.'

'That's kind,' I reply, thinking how there's no way I'd ask that sour-faced woman for any help. Not even if I were dying.

'How many of those have you had, Matt?' Suki asks, inclining her head at his can of lager. 'I thought you were going to go easy.' She turns to Piers. 'He's trying to lose the beer gut, but it's not going too well.'

Matt pats his stomach good-humouredly. 'This baby? I'm trying to cultivate it, not get rid of it.' He and Piers laugh, but Suki just purses her lips.

'You're succeeding,' she says to her husband. 'It's getting bigger by the second. Glad you're feeling better, Mia,' she says to me without enthusiasm before turning away and glaring at Matt until he takes the hint and follows on behind.

'Matt is so whipped,' Piers says to me with a grin. 'Suki needs a slap.'

I'm not inclined to disagree.

I have to put up with another two hours or so of small talk. Music and laughter shuffles in and out of my consciousness until finally everyone leaves and I can flake out on one of the sofas. Piers tries to pull me to my feet, but I resist him, my body heavy and lethargic. I want to stay here in the lounge and curl up on the sofa.

'Come on, Mia,' he says. 'Help me out. I can't carry you all the way downstairs.'

'Staying here,' I mutter, leaning back. My stomach is cramping and the lounge ceiling spins past as though it's on a carousel. Piers leans over me again. He's talking, but I'm not listening, and I suddenly find it hilarious that he doesn't know how much he's annoying me right now. I try to tell him how arrogant he is, but the words won't come out right. Instead, I'm giggling and pointing up at him, jabbing him in the chest.

'Okay, Mia,' he says with a sigh. 'You win. If you want, we can sleep up here tonight.' He flops next to me and sticks his feet up on the wooden coffee table, knocking a can of beer onto the floor. Pale amber liquid seeps onto the carpet, but I don't have a clear enough head to reprimand him.

'Like my mum with the coasters,' I mumble. 'She wouldn't be happy with you.' I poke his shoulder with my forefinger.

Piers turns to me with a heavy-lidded smile. He starts unbuttoning my dress, but I push his hand away, flapping at him, irritated.

'God, you really are pissed,' he says.

'No shit, Sherlock,' I say. Then, I turn away from him, lean over the arm of the sofa and puke my guts up onto the carpet.

'For fuck's sake, Mia. I am not clearing that up.'

I sit back up on the sofa and wipe my mouth with the back of my hand. He glares at me in disgust and I give him what I imagine to be a triumphant smile.

He stands up and steps away from the sofa as if I'm contaminated. 'I'm going to sleep downstairs – in a bed,' he says. 'Are you coming?'

I shake my head.

Piers leaves me and my vodka-induced vomit, his footsteps receding down the stairs. After throwing up once more, my head clears a little and the room stops spinning. I still feel the urge to laugh, thinking how I've discovered the key to getting rid of my boyfriend – a pile of unglamorous puke. Maybe Piers will be so disgusted he'll leave me for good.

CHAPTER SIXTEEN

I wake with a start. It's dark. I must have finally fallen asleep on the sofa. I remember clearing up vomit and then scrubbing at the carpet – which is probably ruined now. My tongue is stuck to the roof of my mouth, a sour taste lingering. Further images of my hellish day flash up in my mind. My sister's sneering face, my mum's tears, the house stuffed with strangers and their pitying gazes, Piers' disgusted expression.

I feel like I should stir myself. Get up and go to bed. But what if Piers is down there? I can't face him. He'll want to sleep with me and I realise the thought repulses me. But, all the same, it's a little creepy up here, alone in the lounge, in the dark with the French windows open, the curtains billowing.

There are no sounds now but the sigh of the river and the boats gently knocking together. I should close the balcony doors, it's not safe to leave them open overnight – anyone could climb up and walk in.

I must have spooked myself, because now I fancy I see a shape out there. It looks like a person, but it can't be. It's surely just my imagination. I should get up off the sofa and close the doors. The hairs on my neck and arms prickle, rising up, a warning of danger. I'm rooted to the sofa. I swear the shape is moving, walking towards me. I want to scream, but my mouth won't open, my throat doesn't work. I don't dare even swallow.

It's not my imagination. It's real. There's someone out on the balcony, coming closer. A woman. The same woman I saw in my dream. She's out there and she's angry. Coming for me, and there's nothing I can do to stop her. Slowly, slowly she walks into the room. It's too dark to make out her features. Just her silhouette. If she ran at me it would be better, it would spur me to action, to scream and run, to lash out. But her steady pace has immobilised me. I know her, but I don't know her. I can't think straight. Her grim expression pins me to the spot.

She's not here to talk.

My stomach lurches in terror and I finally find the muscles I need to open my mouth and scream…

My eyes fly open.

There's no one here.

I didn't utter a sound, but my mouth is open. I close it.

My heart is pounding, my body slick with perspiration.

It was a dream. Just a dream. I'm in the lounge, but there is no woman. There's no one here but me. Just me, in a sweat-soaked nightmare. I lurch to my feet and stumble across to the balcony, closing the French windows with a bang and a shudder of fear. My heart is beating loud enough to wake the neighbours. I have to get out of this room. I know it's ridiculous, but I can't help thinking anyone could be in here, hiding in the shadows, behind the sofa or pressed up against the wall behind the curtains. Watching. Waiting. I'm desperate to run back down the stairs to my bedroom – I don't care if Piers is there or not. I'm going downstairs to my bed where I will sleep with the lights on and the windows closed.

If I can sleep at all.

I don't feel too bad this morning, considering how monumentally awful the weekend was. I spent most of yesterday in bed trying not to think about anything other than what the best cure for a hangover is, and how many paracetamol it's safe to take without straying into overdose territory. But the worst thing was the constant flashbacks to my nightmare which punctuated the whole day. The feelings of terror stayed with me all through my waking hours and into the night. It's the second time I've dreamt about that woman, and I'm praying it will be the last.

Piers left sometime yesterday. We barely said two words to each other all day. I think he wanted me to apologise to him for daring to vomit in his presence. I'm also pretty sure he expected me to be more grateful for the party he arranged. But, as I was barely coherent for most of the day, the most he got out of me was: 'I'm not very good company, you should go home.' To which he didn't reply.

Now, I'm on my way to the rowing club, walking briskly. It's early, but I couldn't lie around in bed this morning. Despite everything that went wrong over the weekend, I'm more positive today, full of a nervous energy that I need to make use of. I don't know if Jack will be there, but I hope so. I want to get out on the water. I need to do something active. Something other than exploring the disaster my life used to be.

Apart from a guy jogging on the far side of the green, oversized headphones clamped to his ears, I appear to be the only person out here. The sun hangs low in the sky, peeping out from a stand of trees on the opposite bank. It's early, so the air is fresh and cool, the scent of damp grass and earthy river making me think of more primaeval times, although the August sun will soon suck all the moisture from the ground – it's going to be another hot one today.

Rummaging around in my wardrobe earlier, I found a shelf with a collection of Lycra shorts, leggings, tops and fleeces. I assumed this must be my rowing gear, so I picked out a pair of navy shorts, a t-shirt and a lightweight tracksuit top. Not sure I'll need the tracksuit, but I don't know how cold it will feel out on the river.

I glance at my watch. Only six twenty. I'm way too early. Jack said he normally goes out at seven. That's okay, I don't mind if I have to wait. I pass the playground and round the bend, crossing the narrow concrete slipway. My pulse quickens in anticipation. I'm nervous about doing this… and about seeing Jack again. He was nice to me last time I came here. Easy-going. Friendly. I hope he won't mind me showing up.

The metal shutters to the boat store are raised. Someone must be here. I hesitate, not wanting to walk inside or call out. I don't know why I feel so nervous. I stand on the path, waiting for someone to appear, wondering if I look as awkward and uncomfortable as I feel, twirling the end of my ponytail and shifting from foot to foot. I should probably be doing some warm up exercises, but I'm too self-conscious.

Voices float out from inside the boatshed. Female voices. My awkwardness vanishes. I'm disappointed that it's not Jack. Two young women emerge, carrying a boat between them, over their shoulders. They lay it on two stands which have already been set up on the shingle. The women can't be more than eighteen or nineteen. Tall and slim, wearing similar clothing to me, but with flip flops, baseball caps and shades. Items I realise I should have brought with me.

'Hey,' one of them says to me with a smile. 'You going out?'

'I'm waiting for Jack Harrington,' I say. 'Is he here yet?'

'Jack?' She glances at her watch. 'He should be here soon. You got a lesson?'

'Not a scheduled one. Just hoping he's free.'

'Okay.' She smiles again.

I sit on one of the oversized rocks that punctuate the edge of the path, and watch the girls as they prepare to go out, hoping to pick up tips. Strangely, it's a ritual that seems familiar. I actually recognise what they're doing, and I also know the name of the equipment they're using. Maybe being here will trigger something and I'll have a real memory. Something that will help me remember who I am.

I turn my head as an Audi Estate pulls into the car park next to the clubhouse. It's Jack.

With a splash, the girls are finally on the water, pulling away quickly.

Jack gets out of his car and raises his hand in a wave. I can't tell if it's to me or the girls in the water, but I wave back anyway. He closes his car door and locks it with a beep and a flash of lights.

'Hey, Mia. Coming out?'

'If that's okay?'

'Course.' He walks my way, his Reefs crunching over the loose gravel. He's wearing jersey shorts, frayed at the edges, a Club t-shirt and wraparound sunglasses. 'Want to go in a double?'

'I'm not sure,' I say. I'm pretty sure he's referring to a boat that will take two of us.

'No,' he says, stuffing his car keys into his gym bag. 'Let's take out two singles instead. I'm betting you can remember what to do.'

We get the boats out in companionable silence. Jack was right – I do know what to do. It feels like second nature, leaving the shore and following him out into the centre of the river, leaving our footwear lying exposed on the bank. It's calm and quiet out here, just the water buffeting the splash guard and the warm breeze rippling over my skin. After ten minutes or so, I feel the tingle of blisters forming on the fleshy pads beneath my fingers. I realise that rowing is how I must have got the callouses on my palms.

'That's it, Mia,' Jack calls out from in front. 'Keep your back straight, and push down with your legs.'

I do as he instructs, and feel the boat surge. 'Thanks!' I reply.

We pass the sailing club, and the cluster of mews houses where I live. I'm too busy concentrating on my stroke to look out for my house. Soon, the river widens out into the harbour. There are fewer boats moored up and it feels like we're heading into a more natural habitat. Just the river bordered by thick hedges and trees – poplars, willows and evergreens – the sky above us and the water below.

This is just what I need to clear my head. My heart pumping, my muscles burning.

'Had enough yet?' Jack calls out.

'No way.'

Although I seem to know what I'm doing, I still feel the need to concentrate. I'm scared of falling in – aside from the embarrassment, the river is dark below, and I'm betting it's cold and deep, infinite. I wonder if this is where I capsized last week. I shake off the thought. It's a beautiful day, and I'm out with a friend – an experienced coach. I'll be fine. But I can't repel the sense of unease that's creeping over me. My eyes are drawn by the inky darkness, wondering if this is the spot where I went into the water. Questions assail me. Did I tip in suddenly? Was I scared? Was I alone, struggling to reach the bank? Or was someone with me? Was it really just an accident? How did I end up on Southbourne Beach? It seems strange that I was swept all the way downriver into the bay. Did I manage to swim all that way?

I imagine myself thrashing and flailing, struggling for breath. I could so easily have been taken under by the strong currents. Pulled into the murky depths. Sucked down by the greedy ocean.

'Mia… Mia, are you okay?' Jack's voice breaks through my panic. I hear him as though from a long way away. It's like my ears are blocked with water. Almost as if I'm down there, straining to hear through the rippling layers of the river. I'm breathing too shallowly. Unable to catch my breath, like a repeating rhythm I can't break out of. Rasping. Gasping. My fingers tingling. My head tight and woozy. Am I about to faint like I did the other night?

'Mia, don't let go of the blades. I don't want you going in.'

I hear Jack's voice and tighten my grip, my blades hanging heavy in my hands. His face comes into focus.

'It's okay, Mia,' he says. 'You're safe. I'm here with you.' His face blurs again. 'Look at me.' I do as he says and refocus on him. His eyes are concerned, gentle. 'Here,' he says. 'Drink this.' He throws his water bottle into my boat and it lands below my seat. I manage to take both blades in one fist and retrieve the bottle with trembling hands. 'You might have a touch of heatstroke,' he says. 'That sun is already pretty strong.'

As the chilled water passes my lips, I begin to feel a little less dizzy and panicked. Maybe he's right. Maybe I'm just dehydrated.

'How are you feeling now?' he asks. 'Any better?'

A flash of green water and rising bubbles. The pull of the darkness. The river in my lungs. And then, I'm suddenly back in the sunshine. Tugged into the present once more. With Jack. With the friendly blue of the sky above, and the rustle of the trees around us. The comforting sounds of the morning now clear and defined. The air has lost that muffled quality and I no longer feel like I'm underwater.

'I'm sorry,' I say. 'I'm not sure what happened.'

I see relief on Jack's face, a concerned smile. 'You look much better,' he says. 'I was really worried for a moment. You looked so out of it, like you were going to pass out. Do you want to get out now? We can walk back and I can pick up the boats later.'

'No, I'll be fine. I might have to take it a bit easier on the way back, though.' I'm starting to feel a little foolish for getting so worked up. I'm not sure what just happened. It was as though I was in another time and place for a few moments. A dark, scary time and place. What must Jack think of me?

'Are you sure?' he says. 'You shouldn't overdo it. Not with heatstroke.'

'Honestly, I'm okay. That drink of water really helped. Just got a little dehydrated,' I lie.

He's frowning at me. Chewing his lip. I pity the poor man having to put up with me being such a drama queen. I smile to reassure him. 'I promise, I'm absolutely fine now.' I start moving off, turning my boat around, so Jack has to follow.

When we get back, the clubhouse looks busier, with groups of rowers out front, and the car park filling up. My legs are jelly once we're back on land, and I don't think it's anything to do with my level of fitness. We don't have to put our boats away, as there are more rowers waiting to take them out. A few people greet me by name. I smile and say hello, but thankfully they don't ask me about the accident or my memory. I don't think I could handle any questions from more people I don't recognise right now.

Jack and I stand a little awkwardly on the path by the boat shed.

'Shall I walk you back home?' he asks. 'Or, if you want company, we could get some breakfast? I don't have to be at work till later today.'

His offer takes me aback, but I realise I really don't want to be on my own right now. 'Thanks,' I reply. 'Breakfast sounds really good. I'm starving.'

'Not here, though,' Jack says. 'I'll get roped into doing club stuff. Let's go into town.'

CHAPTER SEVENTEEN

Jack and I head away from the river, along the quiet back streets. We pass rows of bungalows and chalets until we reach the older part of town with its tiny terraced cottages.

'Apart from your dizzy spell, it seemed like you enjoyed that,' he says as we walk.

'I loved it. If my legs weren't so shaky, I'd want to go straight back out.'

Jack laughs and I smile back at him.

After five minutes or so, we reach the High Street. It's jammed with pedestrians and rush-hour traffic. It feels decadent to be going out for breakfast while everyone else is heading to work.

'Over there.' Jack points to a café on the opposite side of the road. We sidestep traffic, getting beeped by an angry guy in a Mercedes. Jack doesn't get riled, though. He takes my hand, waving at the car as he guides me across the road. I feel a ring on his finger. Glancing down, I see it's a wedding ring. I don't know how I never noticed it before. My heart gives a thud of disappointment. He lets my hand go once we're back on the pavement.

'That traffic was a bit hairy,' I say.

'Yeah, downtown Christchurch can be brutal on a Monday morning.' He grins and opens the door to the café. I scoot in under his arm. The place has only just opened, and the staff are still setting up.

'Jack!' A guy comes out from behind the bar area, and claps him on the back.

'Alright, Chris. How's it going?'

'Good, man, good. I'll be down the club later. You been out?'

'Yeah, it's perfect out there today. You know Mia, right?'

'Sure. Hi, Mia. How was the water?'

'Great, thanks.'

'Awesome. You guys here for breakfast?'

We nod and chat a little more as Chris seats us at a table in a sunny courtyard out the back. But my eyes are drawn upward. The courtyard is set at the base of a grassy hill, and at the top sits a grey stone ruin. It looks ancient. It doesn't seem real.

'That's so cool,' I say. 'What is that place?'

'That's the castle ruins. We can go up there after, if you like?'

'Really?'

'Yeah, sure. It won't take long.'

We order fresh orange juice, coffee, and a proper fry up – eggs, bacon, mushrooms, fried bread – the lot. We don't have to wait long for our food to arrive, and it's absolutely mouth-wateringly delicious. Jack smiles as I sigh with pleasure.

'Glad to see it's hitting the spot.'

'I don't think I've had one proper meal since my accident,' I reply. 'This is like heaven.'

'No one feeding you up?' he says. 'What about Piers? Isn't he looking after you?'

'Do you know Piers?'

'Not very well. But I've met him a few times at some of our race weekends and club nights.'

'Oh, yeah, of course.' I want to ask him about his wife, but it sounds a bit forward, so I don't. 'Piers is finding all this a bit hard. My amnesia, I mean.'

'I guess it's rough on both of you.'

'You could say that.'

'And… Can you really not remember anything from before?' Jack stares at me. His blue-green eyes vivid against his tanned face. 'You don't have to talk about it if you don't want.'

'Well,' I reply. 'At least I can remember how to row.'

He laughs. 'You were great out there, today. Picked it up like a pro.'

'Thanks. It felt great. It's the best I've felt since the accident.'

'Good. You'll have to keep it up.'

'I'll make sure to bring water and a hat next time.'

He's already finished his food, but I'm only halfway through mine. 'Sorry, looks like I'm a slow eater,' I say.

'It's better for you to eat slowly. I scarfed mine down like an animal, I should be the one apologising.'

I feel more relaxed here with Jack than I ever do with Piers. We're easy in each other's company. And it doesn't hurt that he's gorgeous looking. But in an understated way, rather than Piers' slick, groomed handsomeness. I know it's unfair to compare, but I can't help it. Jack has charisma. Anyway, I don't know why I'm even thinking like this. He's married. Off-limits. So I'd never act on these feelings.

My phone pings. It's a text from Piers asking what I'm doing today. I'll reply to it later. I can't go on like this, dreading his calls and visits. However good we were before the accident, we're certainly not right for each other any longer. I've given it a week, and I can't stand it anymore.

I finally finish my breakfast, defeated by half a slice of fried bread.

'Lightweight,' Jack teases.

He offers to pay for breakfast, but I won't let him, so we agree to split the bill, leaving a large tip. Back outside, the traffic has eased, but the pavements are heaving with impatient shoppers and slow-moving tourists.

'Turn right,' Jack says.

I do as he says and we wind our way, single file through the crowds. We turn right again at the roundabout, and here, at last, the crowds thin out. I recognise the French restaurant where I had lunch with Piers last week. That day seems like months ago. Jack guides me down a little pathway where I'm surprised to see some wooden stocks.

'Are those real?' I ask.

'Yeah. I was put in them as a kid. Had rotten fruit thrown at me all afternoon. Scarred me for life.'

'No!' I turn to him in disbelief.

'No,' he confirms.

I give him a light shove. 'I actually believed you for a second.'

'They're just a replica of the real thing,' he says. 'Must have been uncomfortable and humiliating to be stuck in there all day. And that was the whipping post.' He points further along to an unremarkable looking wooden post.

I shudder at the thought of such barbaric medieval punishments.

We continue on along the shady lane. To our left is an immaculate bowling green. Then, straight ahead, I see the grassy hill we saw from the café. It doesn't look quite as astonishing from this angle, but it's still impressive. And at its summit sit the castle ruins.

'Can we go up?' I ask.

Jack nods and I follow him up the steep, curving stone steps which have been carved into the hillside. It only takes us a minute to reach the top. The castle walls are of thick, grey stone, mossy in parts. The roof is missing and most of the walls are crumbling, but there's a pretty view of The Priory and the surrounding houses. I can also see the courtyard where we had breakfast only moments ago. A young family is seated there now, studying menus.

'I wonder who destroyed the castle,' I say.

'Cromwell,' Jack replies. 'What a vandal.'

'How old is it? The castle.'

'Early twelfth century. Almost a thousand years old. Amazing really.'

'Are you into history?' I ask.

'My wife's a history teacher,' he says. 'She loves all this stuff.'

I feel an irrational twinge of envy.

'Does she like to row, too?' I ask.

'She loves it,' he says. 'Because of her work, she doesn't get to go out as often as she'd like.' But there's something in his voice I can't place. Like he's distracted by something. 'You ready to go back down?'

'Yeah, sure,' I reply. But I'm not. I feel like I could stay up here with him for the rest of the day. I don't want to go back down to face reality. Not at all.

CHAPTER EIGHTEEN

It's lunchtime but I'm not hungry. Probably something to do with the insanely huge breakfast I had this morning with Jack. But my lack of appetite is also down to worry. I'm out on the balcony trying to relax, but I can't settle. It's as though I'm riding a never-ending rollercoaster, my stomach constantly swooping and rising. There are too many things to think about, and I don't know what to do about any of them.

This morning, out on the river, was perfect. If I could do that every day, and nothing else, I think I could be content, even if my memories never returned. But there are too many other concerns tugging at me. It feels like there's someone tapping on my forehead, slowly and steadily wearing on my nerves. I shift my legs and bottom, trying to get comfortable on the lounger, but the sun is too hot, my brain is racing, my body on edge. It still feels like I'm living in someone else's house, inhabiting someone else's life.

This is no good. I'm not going to be able to lie here. I need to do something. I sit up, swing my legs off the lounger, and sit for a moment, resting my chin on the heel of my hand. Finally, I stand, rolling my neck and shoulders from side to side. They're stiffening up a little after this morning's rowing session. I pad inside, pulling the balcony doors closed behind me. As I do so, I get a momentary flashback of the woman from my nightmare. Her anger. Her slow walk towards me. I push the image away and swallow down a spark of fear.

My mouth is dry, so I head over to the kitchen and turn on the tap, waiting a few moments until it runs cold. I reach up to one of the cupboards to get a glass. No, that's where the plates are kept. I still don't know my way around my own kitchen. I open another cupboard where a few packets and tins rest forlornly on the shelves. Anger wells up inside me, tears forming behind my eyes. This is ridiculous. I can't cry simply because I forgot which cupboard I keep the glasses in. I yank open another cupboard door. The glasses sit there, glinting, mocking. The urge to smash them rushes through me. But I don't. Instead, I take one out and hold it under the gushing water. Fill it to the top and then gulp the whole lot down. My hand is shaking, but I will not give into my anger and sadness. I turn off the tap, place the glass carefully on the drainer, and curl my hands into fists to stop them trembling.

I must distract myself with something. Something useful. I leave the lounge and go downstairs. As I descend to the ground floor, the air becomes pleasantly cooler. I push open the door to the office, cross the room and fire up my laptop. I tap in a search for PC repair shops. After a few minutes scrolling and clicking, I find a place not too far away. I consider giving them a call first, but then change my mind. I need to get out of the house.

Glancing around the office, I soon see what I'm looking for on the floor, propped up next to the filing cabinet – a grey neoprene laptop bag. I close the machine, unplug it and slide it into the bag, along with the power cable.

Twenty minutes later, I park up outside a tiny shop imaginatively named *The PC Repair Shop,* squashed in between a sandwich place and a key cutters. It's a no-parking zone, but I won't be long. I grab my bag from the passenger seat and leave the Mini's cool interior for the blazing midday heat. Two steps later and I push open the door to the shop, setting a bell jangling above my head. It's warm and musty in here, the faint scent of electrical wires and circuits in my nostrils.

'Coming!' a man calls out from a back room somewhere. He appears moments later through a half-open frosted glass door. 'Mm, sorry,' he says, wiping crumbs from the corners of his mouth. 'Just grabbing some lunch.' He's in his forties, greying hair, friendly looking. 'Can you believe this summer we're having?'

'I know,' I reply. 'It's like the Mediterranean out there.'

'Too hot to be working,' he says. 'Anyway, how can I help?'

'Just wondering if you're able to retrieve deleted emails?'

'From your laptop?' he asks, inclining his head at my bag.

I nod.

'Depends on your email provider… and other things. Best thing is to leave it with me. I'll take a look and see if it's possible. Is it one particular email you're missing?'

'No. All of them. I've only got the ones that were sent to me this week. The rest have all been deleted somehow and I need to get them back. The "sent" ones, too.'

'Okay. Well, as I said, leave it with me and I'll do my best to find them for you.'

'Thanks. Do you know how long it might take?'

'Hard to say. Give me your number and I'll give you a call as soon as I know one way or the other.'

'Do you think you can do it?' I ask. 'What are my chances?'

'Truthfully, you've only got a ten to twenty percent chance of getting them back. You could be lucky – I might snag a few of them.'

'Okay. Thanks.'

I spend the next five minutes filling out paperwork, and he gives me a receipt which I stuff in my purse. I leave the shop just in time, by the look of it, as I spy a traffic warden up ahead, walking purposefully towards my car. I hop in, start up the engine and pull away. The warden wags her finger at me with a smile, as I drive past. I smile back and shrug my shoulders.

That's one chore out of the way. But now I have something far more unpleasant to do.

*

I hear him coming up the stairs. I grit my teeth, waiting, sitting on one of the kitchen stools dipping a carrot baton into a tub of hummus. He smiles as he walks over to me, a bouquet of pink roses in his arms. *Too late for flowers*, I think, shoving the carrot in my mouth and chewing hastily.

'Hey, babe.' He leans in to kiss me on the lips, then presses the bouquet into my hands. His aftershave masks their scent.

'Hi. Thanks, they're beautiful.' I lay them on the counter.

'So are you.'

He's not making this easy.

'Piers…'

'Want a drink? It's not too early is it?' He looks at his watch. 'Four thirty. I think we can crack open a bottle of something cold. Got any white in the fridge?'

'Rosé.'

'That'll do.'

Maybe I *will* have a glass. It might make this less difficult.

'You should put those flowers in water,' he says. 'They'll die in this heat.'

'In a minute.'

As he strides round to the fridge, I watch him. His outfit is immaculate as usual – one of his many pairs of beige shorts and pale blue shirts. It's one of the things that irritates me about him. I feel bad for what I'm about to do. He's obviously trying to make things up with me after our crappy weekend, even if he hasn't actually apologised. I get the feeling he doesn't realise he's done anything wrong. He thinks he's been supportive – coming round here all the time, organising the party. Maybe it's my fault. Maybe I'm the one with the problem. Either way, it's not working and I have to end it. I need space and time to figure out who I am. I'll have a glass of wine first. Dutch courage.

Piers locates the wine glasses without any of the problems I had earlier. Opens the right cupboard first time. *Well done, Piers.* I'm being a bitch in my head. I need to stop it. He fills each glass to the brim, half emptying the bottle.

'Got anything else to dip in the hummus?' he asks.

'Celery? More carrots?'

'Yeah, okay,' he says without much enthusiasm.

I go to the fridge and take out a packet of ready-prepared veggies, slide them onto a plate, grab the hummus, and follow him out to the balcony. But then I stop. Things might get heated in a minute, and I don't want the neighbours to hear.

'Can we sit inside?' I say.

'I've been inside all day,' he says. I hear the scrape of furniture as he repositions the chairs to face the sun.

'Okay.' I acquiesce.

He takes a gulp of wine. 'Ah, that's better. How was your day? You look good. Been out in the sun? You've got a few freckles, babe.' He touches the tip of my nose with his finger. 'Cute.'

My nerves return, but I can't chicken out of this. We're not right for each other. I know it, even if he doesn't. I wonder if maybe I'd already realised this before my accident. I take a sip of wine. It's cold and crisp with a hint of sweetness, but I'm not enjoying it. I set my glass back on the table.

'Piers,' I begin.

He smiles across at me, a look of lazy lust in his eyes.

'Piers, this past week has been… difficult.'

'You can say that again. You're feeling better, though, aren't you? Apart from the whole memory loss thing.'

'Kind of,' I say. 'But, the thing is, losing my memory has meant that I'm starting all over again. With everything. I don't know any of the people in my life. I don't remember our history, or what drew us together.'

'You're talking about us, right?' he says, putting his glass on the table. 'You and me?'

'You, me, my family, my friends.'

He leans forward. 'I'll help you through it, Mia. I can tell you everything you need to know. I love you, babe. I'm here for you.'

'But that's just it,' I say. 'I don't think I want to be told. I think I want to rediscover it all for myself. Start again, if you like.'

'Why don't I move in here?' he says, not taking the hint. 'It'll be easier. We can rediscover everything together... if you know what I mean.' He grins.

'No,' I say. 'I think... I need to be on my own.'

'Okay. Well, I don't have to move in.' His smile disappears. He's offended.

'Piers, you're not listening.' I look into his eyes with the most serious expression I can muster. 'I want to be on my own.'

He stares back, finally understanding. 'Without me, you mean.' He tilts his head and chews the inside of his cheek.

I don't reply.

'What happens when you get your memory back and you realise you've made a mistake?' he says. His voice isn't pleading. It's hard.

'I guess I'll have to take that chance.'

'So that's it then? We're finished?' he says, shaking his head, disbelieving.

'I'm sorry.'

'Well, that's just fucking great isn't it.' He stands up and downs his wine. 'That knock on the head really screwed up your brain, Mia. You've been weird ever since the accident. I'm the best thing that's ever happened to you, and you're chucking it all down the drain. I was going to ask you to... Oh, what's the point. You're going to regret this.' He shoves past my chair and walks back inside. I stand up and follow him, trying to ignore my trembling body, and keep it together. I knew this would be hard, but it's awful seeing him so bitter and angry.

'I'm sorry, Piers. I didn't want to hurt you. I… It's just not right between us.'

'And what about the business?' he says. 'The new apartment's in both our names. What about all the work I've put into it?' He runs both hands through his hair.

'I don't know,' I reply. 'We'll work something out. You can buy me out or something.'

'Yeah, like you need the money,' he mutters. His face twists. 'For someone so loaded, you're a tight cow.'

'Charming,' I say, taken aback by his bitterness.

He's standing at the top of the stairs, his face red, his perfect hair messed up for once. 'Mia,' he says with disgust. 'You really are a complete bitch.'

His reaction confirms that I've made the right decision. This man isn't kind or thoughtful or caring. He's angry and mean, with no empathy for my situation. And what's worse – he's more concerned about the business than about me.

He turns away, his footsteps recede, the front door slams. Through the French windows, I hear his car start up, the engine revving hard. The squeal of tyres as he leaves.

I'm shaking, but it's done.

CHAPTER NINETEEN

Another early morning, and I'm on my way to the rowing club again. Excited to get back out on the water and – if I'm honest – to see Jack. I can hardly believe I'm finally free of Piers. That he won't be coming around anymore. But my relief is tinged with guilt. I honestly hadn't wanted to hurt him, despite how he reacted.

As I round the bend, my heart lifts as the clubhouse comes into view, along with the sight of Jack setting up the boat stands. He glances up and smiles.

'Hey. You coming out again?' he says.

'If that's okay?' I reply.

'Course it's okay.'

'Look, I've got a baseball cap, and my own water bottle today.' I wave it around for him to see. 'I reckon one more session out there with you, and then I'll be good to go out on my own. I don't want to be a nuisance.'

'Mia, it's fine. I'm happy to go out on the water with you whenever you want.'

'Thanks.' I feel heat in my face and hope he hasn't noticed.

We stay out for an hour or so, until Jack says he has to get back for a training session with some of the juniors. It's been another heavenly morning. Peaceful. Nothing but the hiss and splash of the blades, and the occasional quacking of ducks. I suddenly realise that I'm dreading going back home. Panic bubbles up inside me. I don't know what I'm supposed to do for the rest of the day. There's nowhere I have to be. Nothing I have to do. Nobody who needs me. I am completely on my own – apart from my follow-up hospital and therapy sessions. I wish I could just keep rowing. But that won't solve anything. I need to go back and face my fears. Start living my life. But how? I don't know where to begin.

We reach the bank and begin lifting our boats out onto their stands. It's even hotter off the water and I'm glad I remembered a hat today. No one else is around, just the odd dog walker along the footpath. Jack's juniors will be here soon, but for now, it's just us. He heads up to the clubhouse, brings the hosepipe down and throws me a cloth.

'I'll hose the boats, you clean,' he says, as water spurts out of the pipe.

I do as he asks and start wiping down my boat.

'Want to go out for a drink later?' Jack asks. 'Nothing funny.' He grins. 'Just friends. I don't want Piers to beat me up.'

It scares me how much I would like to go out for a drink with Jack. But he's married. Wouldn't it be inviting trouble? Maybe. But I'm lonely, and I could really do with the company of someone I actually like. I've only known Jack for a day or two, but he's the closest to a friend I've got. 'Actually, Piers and I broke up yesterday.'

'Oh,' he says.

'It's fine,' I say. 'We weren't really getting on.'

I look up and catch his eye. He looks taken aback, like he doesn't know what to say. Maybe he only asked me out for a drink because he knew I was already with someone, and his wife wouldn't mind. Being suddenly single now might make it awkward. I should let him off the hook.

'Won't your wife mind us going out?' I say. 'Maybe she could come, too.' Why the hell did I just say that? The last thing I want is to go out for a drink with a loved-up couple, especially when one of them is a complete stranger.

'Funny you should say that about you and Piers,' Jack says. 'Because me and Lucy split up recently, too.'

My pulse quickens. 'I'm sorry to hear that.' I rub hard at a stubborn black mark on the side of the boat. I wonder why he's still wearing his wedding ring if they're not together anymore.

'Maybe we can cry on each other's shoulders.' His voice is melancholy, tinged with bitterness, and I find myself wanting to break through his barriers. To give him comfort. I can't deny the attraction I feel for him. The sensation that something unseen is drawing us together. That I couldn't pull away, even if I wanted to.

The pub garden is crowded, but I spy Jack at a table near the fence, sipping a pint. He spots me and waves, beckoning me over. He stands and kisses me on the cheek. His skin is warm, he smells of water and soap.

'You look good,' he says.

'Thanks.'

'What do you want to drink?' he asks.

'That's okay, I'll get it.'

He looks at me with a smile. 'Sit down,' he says. 'What do you want?'

'Okay, thanks, I'll have a beer,' I say. 'A bottle of something.'

'Becks?'

'Yeah, anything's good.'

'Be back in a minute.'

I slide onto the bench and watch him disappear inside, trying not to focus on how good he looks in his jeans and a navy t-shirt. I've been nervous about this evening all day, but at least it's kept my mind off other stuff. I spent half the day chewing my nails, pacing from one room to the other, and the other half figuring out what to wear tonight. In the end, I settled on a patterned maxi dress with strappy sandals. I was going for boho chic, but now I feel a little overdressed. Everyone else here is in jeans, or shorts and t-shirts. I don't know why I've made this evening into such a big deal. Jack already told me this was a drink "as friends". It's not a date, so I should just relax and enjoy myself.

He's back within minutes.

'That was quick,' I say. 'The bar was heaving when I walked past.'

'Ah, but I know most of the bar staff,' he says with a grin, putting a bottle of beer and a glass in front of me.

'Thanks. I get the feeling that everyone knows everyone in this town,' I say, ignoring the glass and raising my beer bottle in his direction.

'Cheers,' we both say, our drinks clinking.

I take a sip, enjoying the fizz in the back of my throat and the instant buzz that helps to relax me.

'I guess it is a small town,' Jack says, sitting back down. 'A lot of us grew up here, so we do tend to know all the locals. But most people are pretty laid back and friendly.'

'Did you know me very well… before?' I ask.

He looks at me with a half-smile. 'It must be so strange for you, not remembering anything. I still can't get my head around it. But, yes, I knew you before… your accident. We all hung out together at the club. Like you said earlier – everyone knows everyone.'

'And now I have to try and get to know everyone all over again.' I study his face, willing myself to recognise him. On anyone else, such short-cropped hair could be seen as thuggish, but Jack looks anything but.

'Poor you,' he says. 'Do you think your memory will come back?'

'I'm beginning to lose hope,' I say. 'It's been over a week now, and all I've had is one tiny flashback.'

'Oh, yeah? Well, at least that's something.'

'I suppose so.'

'Maybe it's a good thing you lost your memory,' he says.

'How do you work that out?'

'Well,' he says, his face becoming more animated. 'Not many people get the chance to start their lives over. Maybe you could reinvent yourself. Discover what it is you really want to do in life. Think about it – you can be whoever you want.'

'It's weird you should say that, because I've been having the exact same thoughts. It's kind of why Piers and I broke up.'

'So, you were the one who finished it?'

I nod. 'I just didn't seem to click with him. I didn't feel like we were meant to be together. I don't know what I was like before, but I must have changed, because I just can't see me and him ever being on the same wavelength.' I want to ask Jack if he thinks I seem any different than before, but it feels too needy. Like I'm fishing for compliments. 'All I do know about myself,' I say instead, 'is that I love to row.'

'Well, that's the most important thing,' he says. 'Shows you have immensely good taste in sports.'

'Absolutely.' We raise our glasses again, and grin stupidly at each other. I have this wonderful, unsettling feeling that I'm getting in too deep here. That I'm letting myself fall too fast. But I can't stop myself.

We spend the evening in the pub garden, drinking, chatting and laughing. I'm so relaxed in his company. Everything is light and easy. He makes me laugh, and I feel comfortable in my skin for a change. The sky slowly darkens, and the outside lights blink on one by one. It's still warm, but the air has become thick and heavy. The landlord rings a bell and calls last orders at the bar.

'I think there's a storm coming,' Jack says. 'Probably be too choppy to row tomorrow.'

'D'you think?' I ask. 'The river looked so calm on the way here.'

'It won't be like that for long. We should go,' he says, draining his drink. 'Pretty sure it's going to start pouring any minute.'

Jack is right about the storm. A streak of forked lightning suddenly illuminates the garden. Everyone outside gasps, laughs, screams. Seconds later, a boom of thunder cracks above our heads. We follow the crowd back into the pub. Some people stay inside, finishing up their drinks, but many of us spill out into the street as the first plump drops of rain begin to splash onto the dusty pavement. Everyone else disperses, but Jack and I step beneath the covered porch of a tea room next door to the pub.

'I'll walk you home,' Jack says.

'No, I'll be fine,' I say. 'I'm only five minutes away. Where do you live?'

'Over the bridge in Tuckton. Not far either, but in the opposite direction.'

'Okay, well, thanks for a lovely evening,' I say, now wishing I hadn't insisted on walking home alone.

'Are you sure you're okay to go back on your own?' he asks again. 'I don't think you should walk home without company.'

Now's my chance, but I wimp out. 'Yes, honestly, I'll be fine. I'll probably run, though, judging by the monsoon on its way.' To echo my point, thunder rolls and lightning flashes, this time simultaneously. The raindrops come faster now, until the clouds finally burst open releasing sheets of water.

'Well, I'd prefer to see you home,' he says. 'But if you're sure... Goodnight, Mia. It was fun getting to know the new you.' He leans over and pushes a stray tendril of hair behind my ear. My skin tingles at the touch of his fingers, my breathing becomes so shallow I can hardly draw breath. I can't stop myself – I lean forward and kiss him. It's electric. I lose myself. The feel and smell of him is intoxicating.

But it's over too soon.

'Mia,' he says.

I can't speak. My heart is pounding and I want to feel his mouth on mine again.

'Mia, we can't.'

I come back to my senses. He has just told me we can't do this. I want to disagree with him, but I stay silent.

'I've only just split up with my wife,' he says. 'It's not a good idea for me and you to... I'm sorry.'

Disappointment crushes me. But I swallow down my feelings and nod. 'Of course. I'm sorry. I don't know what happened.'

'Don't get me wrong,' he says. 'I want to… but, it's just too soon for me.'

'No, no, of course it is,' I say. 'Of course. Same here, with Piers and everything… I'd better go.' I turn to leave, stepping out from the shelter of the porch, the rain instantly drenching me, making me gasp.

'Mia.' He catches hold of my hand, joining me in the downpour. His grip warm, firm. 'Don't let this keep us from being friends,' he says. 'Come rowing with me again this week. It won't be awkward, I promise.'

'Okay,' I say, desperate to leave, my humiliation open and raw. 'Promise?'

'Sure.'

'Say it. Say that you promise.' Jack smiles.

'I promise,' I say, feeling stupid.

'Good. Okay. See you soon.' He lets go of my hand and turns to leave.

I'm absolutely drenched. My heart is clattering against my ribcage and I can barely breathe. I know I should run to get out of this downpour, but I can't make my legs obey me. Instead, I walk as though in a dream, letting the water run in rivulets down my body. My dress clinging to my legs. My skin soaked. My hair plastered to my face.

The thunder and lightning doesn't scare me. It suits my mood. I almost wish the lightning would strike me. What was I thinking? How could I have kissed him? I barely know him, and he already told me about him and his wife recently splitting up. Feelings of humiliation and mortification bloom as I walk along the rain-drenched pavement. A group of young women, about my age, run past, giggling and shrieking. Swearing and laughing, their footsteps echoing away behind me. I'm a total idiot, and there's no way I'll ever be able to show my face at the rowing club again. What the hell must he think of me? I've ruined the only good thing in my pathetic, lonely life.

I reach the end of the High Street and walk toward the Priory in a drunken, depressed, rain-sodden daze. The cobbles are slick with rain and I have to tread carefully in my slippery sandals. I push open the kissing gate, its hinges squeak and groan as I slide through. The Priory stands proudly, unaffected by the downpour, like it has done for the past millennium. Solid and enduring.

The graveyard is deserted apart from a lone woman coming towards me, her blonde hair soaked through. She looks angry. Maybe she just had an argument with someone. I stop dead. I know her. It's the woman from my dream. The one from my balcony. She's coming closer, her face twisted in fury. But she looks so much more than furious – she looks mad. Dangerous. Murderous.

CHAPTER TWENTY

I should turn and run, but I can't move. Terror has me rooted to the spot. Even if I could make myself scream, no one would hear me through the drumming rain and thunder crashes.

The woman is only a few yards away now. I close my eyes. Squeeze them tight. Why don't I turn and run?

'Are you okay?' A woman's voice next to me.

I open my eyes and stare into hers. It's not the woman from my dream at all. Did I imagine her? Am I going mad? This woman is older, with mousy brown hair and she's looking at me like I'm crazy.

'I'm fine,' I say. 'Sorry, just a bit tipsy. The rain and the grave-yard… they must have spooked me.'

'It is a bit creepy here at night,' she says. 'Got far to go?'

'No, I only live a couple of minutes away.'

'Okay, well, take care, love.'

'Thanks. You too.'

She continues on her way. I turn and stare at her departing figure through a veil of rain. She looks nothing like the woman from my nightmare. Nothing at all. I turn back around. My heart is still pounding, my mouth dry. What if the woman from my dream is still here somewhere? She could be hiding behind a tree, or crouched behind a gravestone. Anywhere. I need to get out of this place. I gather up the dripping hem of my dress and start to run through the graveyard, along the rain-slick path, past the crumbling headstones, beneath the distorted shadows of the looming priory. Down the lane I race, into the empty car park with its high stone walls and swaying trees.

I want to scream, but I don't. Instead, I try to hum a tune to give me courage, but with my ragged breath, it sounds more like I'm whimpering in pain, so I stop. Another crack of thunder makes me lengthen my stride, my footsteps muffled by the raging storm. *Almost home. Almost home.* I chant the words like a charm to ward off evil. *Almost home.*

Is she real, that woman? Is she stalking me? Or is she a figment of my imagination? Either way, I can't get my panic under control. I can't keep the image of her at bay. I'm certain she means to do me harm. *Almost home.*

Finally, I reach the gap in the wall which leads to the cobbled path by the stone bridge. I pause for a second to catch my breath, but fear pushes me forward. I clatter across the bridge, and onto the private road which will take me to my front door. My feet crash through puddles, splashing rainwater up my already-soaked legs.

Almost home.

I glimpse the dark river and the swaying shapes of the trees beyond. The boats brought into sharp relief as another streak of lightning illuminates the night.

Almost home.

But what will I do once I *am* home? I can't escape my nightmares. I've seen her in my house before. She has already followed me into my dreams, and onto my balcony. What if she's there, now? What if she never leaves me alone?

I shiver and pull the soft grey cardigan closer to my body. The weather has cooled since the storm the other night. It's still sunny, but gone is the blistering heat from the past ten days. Instead, a chill breeze ripples the surface of the river, tugs at the sailboats' rigging and whispers through the reeds.

As I recall the storm, an image of the woman flashes into my mind, but I shove her away into the recesses of my brain. I don't let myself dwell on her. If I let her in, she'll trigger another "episode" and I can't handle it. I can't handle her. I wish I could lock her away forever, whoever she is.

I lean forward and reach for my coffee, cradling the mug in my hands as I gaze down at the comings and goings beneath my balcony. It's a perfect morning for sailing, and the river is busy. I wonder what Jack's doing. I haven't seen him since the night of the storm when I made a first-class idiot of myself. I'm realising that it was probably a pity date anyway. He felt sorry for me because of my amnesia thing, and then I went and ruined our new friendship by drinking too much and behaving like a needy fool. My cheeks redden at the memory.

Now, I have too much time on my hands. Too much time to think. To over-analyse, dwell and brood. Instead of thinking, I should be doing something. Something constructive and worthwhile. Piers said I used to be a teacher. Maybe I could go back to it? But I can't remember anything about teaching. I wouldn't begin to know how to act around kids. The thought unnerves me. No. I can't do that. My mind keeps jumping back to the fact that I love rowing. But how can I ever go back to the club when Jack coaches there? That's something I'd love to do – coach rowing. I wonder if I could. I'd have to train, but I already have a primary teaching qualification, so maybe it wouldn't be so hard to get qualified as a coach.

I give a little start as a doorbell rings. Is it mine? No. It's next door. Their French windows are also open and I can hear my neighbour – the delightful Suki – on the phone:

'Matt, can you come home? The man from the fence company's here. He's early.'

I can hear Matthew's reply. Suki must have him on speaker-phone.

'I can't come home, I'm at work, Suki. Did you show him the fence?'

'No, he's outside, ringing the doorbell.'

'Well let him in.'

'Matt, I can't! You promised you'd be here. Just ask Darren – he'll let you leave work for twenty minutes. It's an emergency.'

'It's not an emergency, Suki. It's a guy to fix the fence. Please, just open the door to him. I can't leave work to let someone in, not when you're already there. All you need to do is open the door, show him the broken fence and let him get on with it.'

'No, I'm not opening the door,' she says. 'Come home now, or don't come home at all tonight.'

Wow. Suki sounds like a crazy person. I shouldn't really be eavesdropping like this, but I can't help it. She's so loud. I picture her perfect peaches-and-cream complexion and her shiny brown hair. Her disdainful expression. I wonder why she's so reluctant to open the door. Maybe I should go and see if she's okay… but then she'd know I was listening in to her conversation.

The doorbell rings again, followed by a sharp rapping on their front door. I feel like I'm in the middle of a TV drama. Suki seemed so quiet and stand-offish at the party. Now, she sounds terrified. And more than a little unhinged.

'He's still out there, Matt. He won't go away.'

'What's going on with you, Suki? Please, just let him in. We need that fence fixed. I can't come home. I'm working.'

'Well, thanks for nothing, Matt.'

I lean back in my chair as I see a hand reach out and pull next door's balcony doors shut with a bang. What the hell was all that about? After a while, the doorbell stops ringing. I hear a car door slam, an engine start up, and a vehicle drive away. Suki was true to her word and didn't answer the door to the fence guy. Maybe she has anxiety issues. I swig the last of my coffee and stand up, deciding to go back inside. I guess it isn't just me who has problems.

The doorbell rings again. Maybe next door's fence repair guy is back. Or maybe Matt was able to leave work and he's come back to help Suki after all – but why would he need to ring the bell? I shake my head – my day has dissolved into nothing more than speculation about the neighbours. I really must start doing something with my life. But then I realise this time it's *my* doorbell ringing.

Who could it be? My right eye twitches. The best scenario would be a Jehovah's Witness or someone trying to sell me something. Anyone else will just mean trouble. The bell rings again. I must stop being so timid. Maybe I've got more in common with Suki than I thought. I shake myself out of my stupor and go into the lounge. There's an intercom at the top of the stairs, I press the buzzer.

'Hello?' I say.

'Mia? It's Jack.'

My heart begins to pound. What's he doing here?

'Hi,' I say.

'Can I come in?'

'Yeah, I'm upstairs in the lounge – top floor.' I press the buzzer and hear the faint click of the door opening below. What do I look like? I'm wearing jeans, a grey vest-top and a cashmere cardigan. Hair in a messy ponytail. Not too bad. No makeup though and it's too late to go downstairs and smear on some lip gloss. Never mind. There's nothing romantic going on between us, anyway.

I hear his footsteps on the stairs. Relax when I finally see him. His smile puts me at ease.

'Hey, you,' he says. 'Just thought I'd pop by. I couldn't stop worrying about you walking home alone the other night. I knew I wouldn't be able to relax until I saw you were okay.'

'Thanks,' I say. 'You could've texted – saved yourself a journey.'

'It's hardly a journey,' he says. 'But if this is a bad time...'

'No, no, course not. I just meant... thank you. It's sweet of you to check up on me. I'm fine. Apart from getting completely soaked and imagining a ghost woman, I got home fine.' I gesture to one of the kitchen stools. 'Sit down if you like. Do you want a cuppa? Or a cold drink?'

'Whoa,' he says. 'Back up. What do you mean a "ghost woman"?'

'Oh, you know, the usual – walking through a graveyard at night with thunder and lightning and torrential rain. There has to be the obligatory ghost.' I smile, trying to make light of the memory, but an echo of fear darts through me, the same fear I experience every time I see her – or *imagine* I see her.

'You saw a ghost?' he says, raising an eyebrow.

'I don't know,' I reply. I'm beginning to wish I'd never mentioned her. Even thinking about her makes me break out in a sweat.

'You can't just leave it at that,' he says. 'Tell me. What did you see?'

'Do you remember I told you I had a flashback after the accident?'

'Vaguely.'

'Well, I've had the same flashback three times now. Of a woman walking towards me.'

'What – as in like a memory?' he asks, his eyes widening.

'I honestly don't know. It feels like a dream, but a really realistic dream. Like it's actually happening, but then I open my eyes and there's no one there, so I know it can't be real.'

'And the other night?'

'I was walking back through the priory gardens and I saw her coming towards me. It was definitely her, with this scary, angry expression on her face. I was terrified. But when I looked again, it was just some normal woman. She asked me if I was okay and carried on walking.' I don't tell Jack about my absolute terror afterwards. About my mad dash home. He'll think I'm a lunatic. He may already think that. I wouldn't blame him.

'Mia, you're shivering.' He walks over and wraps me in his arms, rubbing my back and shoulders. 'Here, sit down.' He leads me over to the sofa and sits next to me, still rubbing my back.

'Sorry,' I say, tears brimming behind my eyes. 'I think I'm still a bit shaken up by everything. Bet you wish you'd texted now.' I give a strangled laugh.

'Don't be silly. I'm glad I came over,' he says. 'Have you told anyone else about these flashbacks? A doctor or anyone?'

I sniff back my tears, willing them not to fall. 'No. Well, I told the doctor that I remembered the clubhouse, but I didn't mention the girl. Why? Do you think I should mention it? Could it be an actual memory, do you think?'

'I don't know,' he says. 'But I think it's good to talk about these things to somebody. It's not good to bottle stuff up.'

'Yeah, well, I don't have many people in my life at the moment,' I say, regretting the bitter tinge in my voice.

'Piers, you mean?'

'Piers... my mum... my sister. I can't talk to any of them.' I'm now doing my utmost to stop myself crumbling into a sobbing mess. I need to change the subject, quickly.

'You can always talk to me,' he says, squeezing my shoulder.

'Thank you,' I sniff, 'but you don't want to listen to my problems. I'll be fine. It was just the memory of that woman – it unsettled me.' I stare down at my lap, trying to get myself under control.

'Of course. It would unsettle anyone,' he says. 'Hey, how about we go out for a walk? We can pick up a salad or a sarnie from M&S and have a picnic lunch by the river. I don't have any more coaching sessions until later this afternoon.' He bends down so his face is millimetres from mine, trying to make eye contact with me. I look up and we stare at each other for a second before I turn away and rise to my feet, feeling crumpled and unsteady.

'Let me just wash my face,' I say. 'But, yes, lunch by the river sounds lovely, if you're sure you've got time.'

*

Now we're outside, I feel much better. More in control of myself. We walk to the supermarket and battle the lunchtime crowds to grab ourselves a makeshift picnic, shivering by the chiller cabinets. It's a relief to head back out of the store into the warm sunshine. I walk with Jack, not paying any attention to where we're going. Just happy to be doing something other than sitting on my balcony, worrying about my life. We walk across a road bridge, cars zooming past us too fast, and we chat about the weather and rowing and nothing else of any great consequence, which suits me fine. Jack has been a gentleman and hasn't brought up "the kiss", thank goodness. Hopefully, that embarrassing incident is behind us, and we really can concentrate on being friends.

After the bridge, we cross a few busy roads and find ourselves on the opposite side of the river to the rowing club. We pass a café, a kids' crazy golf course and a playground. Further along, it's quieter. More rural. There's no footpath, just the grassy river bank. Consequently, there are no people this far up. Just a few ducks and geese swimming alongside us to check whether we have any food for them.

'Where do you want to sit?' Jack asks.

'Anywhere's good,' I reply.

'Shade or sun?'

'Sun.'

Jack stops walking. 'Here?'

I nod, and we sit facing the river, our legs stretched out in front of us. Jack opens the carrier bag and plunges his hand in, pulling out my feta salad, followed by a bottle of water and a BLT for him. His hand brushes mine as he passes me my food. I'm all too aware of my body, my crush still plaguing me. I wish I could shake it off.

'Not a bad spot,' he says, taking a bite of his sandwich.

'It's beautiful,' I agree.

We sit in silence for a while. Eating, gazing at the river. It's peaceful. This morning's breeze has died away, and I shrug off my cardigan, enjoying the sun's warmth on my arms. My salad is delicious. I hadn't thought I was that hungry, but now I wish I'd bought more food.

'I'm stuffed,' Jack says, putting his empty sandwich packet back in the bag. He pats his stomach. 'Possibly not the best lunch to have before a 5k row.'

'What time's your session?'

'Not for another hour.'

'How did you get into rowing?' I ask, pulling up fistfuls of grass and letting the blades fall through my fingers.

'Me and my sister did it as kids. She stopped, I carried on. Started studying for my coaching qualifications when I was in my early twenties. I love it. Wouldn't want to do anything else.'

'Do you think, maybe, I could train to be a coach? I've been thinking I need to do something, and rowing is the only thing I seem to enjoy.'

'Yeah, why not.' He turns to me and nods. 'I think it's a great idea.'

'Could I pick your brain sometime? Find out the best way to go about it?'

'Sure. I'll come over some time and we'll check out a few courses online.'

'Amazing. Thank you!'

'You're welcome.' He gives me a smile, and holds my gaze longer than he needs to, his eyes softening into something else. But I won't make the same mistake I did last time. No. If Jack wants to take this further, he'll have to make the first move.

As the water from the shower pounds my body, I can't help smiling. It's funny how things can turn around in such a short space of time. At last, I have something exciting to aim for, to work towards. Maybe now I can put the accident behind me and become a normal person again. I hope so. Even if I never regain my memory, I can still have a good life.

After our picnic today, Jack went off to his coaching session. Nothing romantic happened between us, but I have the feeling that it's only a matter of time. I can sense an undeniable spark between us. I don't blame Jack for holding back. He's just come out of a long-term relationship, and I don't want to end up being his rebound. But I can't deny I want to be more than that.

I'm enjoying the hot water as it cleanses me, my legs ache pleasantly, and my feet tingle. I turn off the shower and smooth my soaking hair from my face, squeezing the excess water from the ends. Inside the shower cubicle, steam envelops me. I open the glass door and give a little shiver as the cooler air hits my body. I grab a towel from the shelf and wrap it around me. Then, I take another and begin drying my hair. I think I'll blow dry it for a change tonight.

I open the door to the en suite and step into my bedroom.

'Here she is.' A slurred voice freezes me in my tracks.

I scream.

Someone is sitting on the end of my bed.

CHAPTER TWENTY ONE

'What the fuck, Piers!'

'Had a nice shower, did you? Getting yourself all tarted up for your new boyfriend?'

'What are you doing here? How the hell did you get in? You gave me your keys.'

Bloody Piers has broken into my house. And by the look of him, he's absolutely blind drunk, sitting – or rather, swaying – on the end of my bed, staring at me through glazed eyes.

'Got another set haven't I.' He's tapping himself on the forehead with his forefinger to indicate that he's done something clever.

'Well, you can give them back, and get the hell out. You scared me to death.'

'That was the idea, stupid.' He grins.

'It's not funny. Please leave.'

'Erm… No.'

'I don't believe this,' I mutter. He's totally shitfaced. How am I going to get rid of him? 'Let me get dressed and then we can talk.'

'Go ahead, get dressed.' He flings his hand out, gesturing to me to carry on.

'I'm not getting changed with you in here. If you won't leave the house, then at least go upstairs and wait for me.' If he leaves the bedroom, I can call the police while he's up there. Get them to come and kick him out.

'Nothing I haven't seen before, babe,' he says with a leer.

'For Christ's sake, Piers, what are you even doing here?' I pull my towel closer around me.

'I saw you.' He's pointing at me, his finger outstretched, waggling up and down accusingly.

'Saw me?' I'm confused. 'Saw me where?'

'Saw you at the pub with *him*. With Jack *Wankington* from the rowing club. Looking all cosy together.'

'So? We went for a drink. So what?'

'He's married, you know. Bet he didn't remind you of that.'

'He did, actually. And I can go for a drink with whoever I like. You and I aren't together anymore, Piers.'

'*You and I aren't together anymore, Piers,*' he mimics. 'Bitch.' He stands up. 'Did you shag him?'

'It's none of your business, but no. I told you, we're just friends.'

'I don't believe you.'

'Believe what you want.'

He's glowering at me. My brain is racing, trying to work out if Piers could be dangerous. I'm pretty sure he's harmless, but I can't be certain.

The curtains to my bedroom are closed, but the French windows are open. If I screamed loudly enough, would anyone hear me? Would they come and help? What if I screamed and no one came?

'Piers, please can you leave. You're scaring me.'

'Good! You deserve it.' He lurches to his feet and takes a couple of steps towards my dressing table, lifts the lid off my Art Deco glass jewellery box, and places it carefully down on the table top. He takes out a bead necklace, holds it up and stares at it, then drops it deliberately onto the carpet. Next, he takes out a bracelet and drops that onto the floor, too. One by one, he lifts out pieces of my jewellery and watches them fall onto the carpet. I have no idea what he's doing, but maybe I can make an escape while he's occupied. I glance at the door. 'You hurt me, Mia,' he says.

'I'm sorry,' I reply. 'I didn't want to hurt you.'

'But you did.'

He picks up the half-empty glass jewellery box and hurls it at the bank of wardrobes to my right. As it smashes into pieces, I feel a sharp pain next to my eye. A fragment must have ricocheted and hit me. But I can't worry about that now. I have to get away from him. He's throwing all the contents of my dressing table at the wardrobes now. My hairbrush, mirror, hairdryer, a candle in a glass jar. With each item he smashes, he accompanies it with an insult. 'Bitch! Whore! Slut!'

I sidle towards the door, but before I can get there, Piers strides over to me and grasps my upper arm painfully. 'Where do you think you're going? We haven't finished talking yet.'

'Let go,' I hiss. 'You're hurting me.' His fingers are digging in. Crushing. Bruising.

'Good,' he says. 'It's less than you deserve. *I hate you.*' He leans in towards me, his face up so close I can smell the whiskey on his breath, mingled with sweat and aftershave, feel flecks of saliva on my face as he raves. 'You know, I was glad you lost your memory,' he says. 'I was happy because it meant we could start over again.' He swipes at his eyes with his free hand. 'I didn't *have* to come and claim you, you know. I could easily have left you there.'

His odd choice of words cuts through my fear, piquing my curiosity. 'What do you mean?' I ask, my voice quavering. 'Claim me?'

'I mean,' he says, thrusting his face even closer to mine, so our foreheads touch. 'I mean that after your accident I should never have come back.' He lets go of my arm and pushes me away. 'I should've left you in the hospital to rot. But, I did the decent thing and identified you. I took you back, more fool me.'

I take a step back, letting his words sink in. 'When you say you "took me back", you're not talking about when you took me back home, are you?'

He's looking sheepish now, as though he's let something slip. Said something he shouldn't have. He moves away from me.

Peels back the curtains and stares out of the open windows at the gathering darkness. He has finally calmed down. His anger has been replaced by… something else. I'm sure I could make my escape now, but the truth is gradually becoming clear to me, and I need to find out if my hunch is correct.

'Piers,' I say, 'were we still a couple when you came to identify me at the hospital?'

He doesn't reply. His silence tells me all I need to know. But I need to hear him say it. I need to find out why.

'Piers, answer me.'

'Technically, not quite.'

His anger has totally dissolved, but mine is about to explode. 'What!'

He turns to face me, his hands out, trying to placate me.

I'm outraged. 'You pretended to still be my boyfriend? Why would you… How did you think you would get away with that? What could you possibly…'

'It wasn't like that. We *were* together. We were together for almost a year. I loved you, and you loved me, too.' His voice is whining now, pleading. He goes back to sit on the bed. He doesn't seem as drunk anymore. Just tired. 'You dumped me the night before your accident,' he says. 'We had a stupid argument about you not wanting to go to the party, and you got cross and said you didn't love me anymore. I didn't think you really meant it. I was sure you'd come around and change your mind, so—'

'So you came to the hospital and pretended I was still your girlfriend. You lied to me. You lied to the police.'

'No.'

I raise my eyebrows.

'Not really,' he says, sounding like a recalcitrant child. 'I thought the police would think it was suspicious – us arguing on the night of your accident. I was scared they would think I was guilty of something. But I had nothing to do with whatever happened to you that night.'

'How do I know that?' I say. 'We could have argued, and you could have tried to hurt me.'

'I would never…'

'Really?' I turn and stare pointedly at the smashed fragments of my possessions strewn on the carpet and all along one side of my bed. At the freshly made dents and scratches on my wardrobe doors. Piers moves towards me, reaches his hand out to my head, but I flinch back and knock his hand away. 'Get the fuck away from me,' I snap.

'I was just going to… You've got blood on…'

I glare at Piers, warning him off. Then, I raise my fingers to the side of my head and gingerly feel around with my fingertips until they come to rest on a splinter of glass embedded near my eye. I pull the splinter out and take a look. It's tiny. I can hardly see it, covered as it is in beads of shiny blood. My fingers are dripping, and I feel it trickle down the side of my face, warm and wet.

'I'm sorry.' He bows his head. 'You have to believe me that I would never willingly hurt you, Mia.'

I give a short bark of laughter. 'You just embedded a piece of glass in my head, you tosser. You broke into my house acting like a fucking maniac, and you just admitted we weren't together when you came to the hospital pretending to be my boyfriend. If I called the police right now, they'd arrest you and you'd deserve it. In, fact, I think I will. They'll slap a restraining order on you, then you won't be able to come near me again.' A fresh rage is building inside me. Fury at Piers for everything he's put me through.

'I'm sorry, Mia.' He's backing away from me now, his face red, his eyes wide and scared.

Good, he deserves to be scared. I've put up with enough shit from him. This is just about the final straw.

'Please don't call the police,' he whines. 'I'll go… I'll…'

'Why shouldn't I call them? You lied to them, and you just assaulted me. Then you can see what it's like to have nothing in your life make sense. To be scared of everything and everyone. To be alone.'

'Mia! No!'

'Yes!' I cry. I feel as though I've lost control of myself. All I want to do is wound him for his crass, insensitive, violent behaviour. How dare he come into my house and try to intimidate me. How dare he. 'Yes, you arrogant prick. You can go to jail. Maybe that way I wouldn't have to come home and find you in my house all the frigging time.'

'They wouldn't believe you,' he says. 'You're acting insane. Your memory isn't reliable. Mia… please.'

I gaze dispassionately at the fearful expression on his face. My shoulders slump. Of course I'm not going to ring the police, but he's certainly done enough to get their attention. He deserves to be scared, like he scared me. 'How do I know you didn't try to hurt me when I finished with you? How can I trust you, Piers? Especially after tonight.'

'I swear I was nothing to do with whatever happened to you that night. You dumped me and I left. Got blind drunk and went to that stupid party. I was heartbroken. I still loved you. I wanted to be with you.' He looks up at me, his eyes bloodshot. 'I still love you, now. I do. Even now. After everything you've said and done.'

'After everything *I've* said and done?' I give a dry laugh. 'You lied to me. You tricked me into believing I was still your girlfriend. Not to mention breaking and entering here tonight and scaring me half to death. Oh, and smashing up my stuff, and insulting me. Feel free to let me know if I've left anything out. No?… Okay. Fine. Now get the hell out of my house.'

'Mia, please.'

'I said, get out!' I'm yelling now. 'And don't come back. *Never* come back.'

As he rises to his feet, I hold my hand out. 'Keys,' I snap. He digs into his pocket and pulls out a bunch of keys, fumbling to slide some of them off the metal keyring. Finally, he drops the set into my palm.

'Are you going to call the police?' he snivels.

'I don't know,' I reply. 'That depends on whether or not you leave me the fuck alone.'

'What about the business? The apartment?'

'Get out, Piers.'

I follow him down the stairs. When we reach the front hall, he turns back towards me, a mournful expression on his face. I glare at him, feeling no pity, and watch as he opens the front door and leaves. I slam the door behind him. I'd be happy if I never had to set eyes on Piers Bevan-Price again, for as long as I live.

I'm still trembling with anger as I tramp back up the stairs. My feet are freezing. I need to dry my hair and put some warm clothes on. I can't believe what just happened. I reach the landing and open the door to my bedroom…

What a mess. I want to cry. Instead, I walk into the en suite. The steam has dissipated and I'm able to look into the magnifying mirror to examine the cut on my head. The blood has dried in a streak down the side of my face. I bring my fingers up to the wound, checking to see if there's any glass still embedded in the skin. It feels okay. I open cupboards and drawers until I find a pack of cotton-wool pads. I clean the cut, trying not to give into the tears brimming behind my eyes. If I start crying now, I don't think I'll ever stop.

As I dab at the wound, I'm interrupted by the doorbell. My hand freezes – cotton wool pad hovering over one eye. What now? Surely Piers wouldn't dare come back. I was pretty clear about him never showing his here face again. Should I ignore it? It rings again. Now someone's banging on the door. I sigh and take a deep breath.

I will march downstairs, deal with whoever is at the front door, then I will come back, clean up my bedroom and pretend tonight never happened. I exchange my damp towel for a dressing gown, and head back down the stairs. I slide the chain across, to prevent anyone forcing their way in. And then, I open the door.

CHAPTER TWENTY TWO

I peer out through the crack in the door, scared of who might be out there, but too curious not to answer it. The security light illuminates a man dressed in sweatpants and a t-shirt, a concerned look on his face. He looks vaguely familiar, but I can't quite place him.

'Hi Mia,' he says. 'I'm just checking to see if everything's okay. We heard shouting and some… noises.'

As soon as he begins talking, it clicks with me who he is. I close the door, slide the chain out of its slot and re-open the door. The cool night air creeps inside and chills me further.

'Hi Matt,' I say to my neighbour, trying to keep my teeth from chattering, wondering what on earth he must be thinking. 'Sorry about all that, before. I'm fine. I just…' There's no point in lying to him, they probably heard every word. '… I had an argument with Piers. He's gone now. Hopefully for good.'

Matt puts his hand out toward my head. 'You're hurt. Did he do that? Should I call the police?'

'God, no. I'm fine. It looks worse than it is. It was an accident.' I realise how that sounds. Like I'm covering up for Piers. I guess it was his fault, but at least it was an indirect injury, rather than an actual physical attack.

'Are you sure? Do you want to come over to ours? You look like you could do with a cup of tea, or maybe a glass of something stronger.'

'I…'

'You're shivering,' he says. 'You must be in shock.'

His kindness will be the unravelling of me. 'No… I'm fine, honestly.' Even as I say the words, I hear the crack in my voice and feel a tear escape from the corner of my eye. The salt stings my cut. Matt steps forward and pulls me into a hug, patting my back in a calming manner, the way I imagine a parent would soothe a crying child. I let myself sink into his bear-like embrace, mumbling about how sorry I am, and how I don't mean to cry all over him.

'I couldn't say so before, but I always thought Piers was a total dickhead,' Matt says.

His words bring a small smile to my face and I sniff, trying to get my emotions back under control. 'You and me both,' I say.

A shape looms behind him and I lift my head a fraction to get a better view.

It's Suki.

I step out from the security of Matt's hug. Suki is immaculate in a fitted dress and a full face of makeup, her dark hair glossy and bouncy, straight out of a shampoo ad. Her face is taut. She must have been unnerved hearing me and Piers yelling like that.

'Hi, Suki,' I say. 'I'm so sorry about the noise. It's nice of you to come over. I was just telling Matt—'

'Just because you can't keep hold of your own man,' she interrupts, 'there's no need to make a play for mine.'

It takes a few seconds for her words to sink in. Did I hear her correctly? I'm stunned into silence. In a caricature of shock, my eyes widen and my jaw begins to drop.

I replay the past few seconds in my mind. There was nothing remotely romantic about Matt's hug. He was simply being kind. How could she have misinterpreted it? I actually can't think of a single thing to say. My tears have dried up and I suddenly have the urge to laugh hysterically at her insane accusation.

'Are you coming, Matt?' she says. 'I told you to leave it alone. It's none of our business what she gets up to. Unless she starts involving you.'

'I'm sorry, Mia,' Matt mumbles.

'Don't apologise to *her*,' Suki says. 'Apologise to *me*.' She turns on her heel and stomps back next door. Matt throws me an apologetic glance and follows her home, like a lapdog.

Did she really just accuse me of going after her husband? I think she must have a screw loose. Honestly, that woman is an absolute nutter. Any sympathy I might have felt for her in the past vanishes.

Matt's so sweet. I have no idea what he's doing married to someone like that. Someone who talks to him like he's nothing. I hear their door close and wish I had never come down to open mine. I should have ignored the doorbell and tried to salvage some of my evening. But now it's totally ruined. My nerves are shot, what with both Piers' and Suki's attacks. Why can't everyone just leave me alone? I didn't ask for any of them to intrude into my life. I'm too tired and shaken to cry about it.

I stand outside my doorstep, delaying going back upstairs to my ruined bedroom. To the memory of Piers' violent intrusion. I'd almost forgotten his revelation about us having split up before the accident. To think, I had to finish with him *twice*. Once was bad enough – at least I can't remember the first time.

A few yards away, the river gurgles and sighs, sympathising over the awfulness of my evening. I wonder what other dramas the river has witnessed tonight. What other arguments and upsets have taken place on its winding banks. Or maybe it's just me. Maybe it just my life that's such a godawful mess.

I'm up and out early today, in a surprisingly good mood, despite my crazy ex-boyfriend and psycho neighbour. I can't let other people's neuroses get me down. I have enough on my plate without taking on their issues. And anyway, I'm off to the rowing club to see Jack. The thought of him makes my stomach flip. I can't pretend to myself that I'm not interested in him. I am. He's all I think about. I can put up with all the other crap as long as I know he's on my side. He's the only thing that feels right in my life. But, then again, he's only just separated from his wife, and I don't want to complicate things further. That wouldn't be fair.

If it weren't for Jack, I would have no hesitation in selling up and leaving Christchurch for good. Beautiful as it is, I've had too many unnerving experiences here. Maybe sometime in the future, when I'm feeling braver, I could start afresh somewhere else. Maybe even abroad. But I'm letting my imagination spool ahead. For now, I must be content to stay in this pretty town with Jack's friendship.

It's another sunny morning. Chilly and bright. Those sticky, humid days before the storm have melted away. Perhaps this is the start of autumn. The end of summer. I don't mind. I welcome the change. Cool evenings and refreshing early mornings – perfect for rowing. I'm wearing my fleece over my rowing gear, walking briskly to warm up, swinging my arms as I pass the sailing-club car park and cross the stone bridge. *Trip trap, trip trap* – Why has that phrase come into my head? Why is it so familiar? I suddenly recall a children's story about a troll under a bridge. I remember the pictures in the book. *The Three Billy Goats Gruff.* They *trip trapped* over the bridge. Is that cause for celebration? Remembering a story from my childhood? Or maybe it was one I read to my pupils when I was a teacher. Either way, I'll have to mention it to Dr Lazowski when I see her next.

I managed to find the energy to clean up my bedroom last night. It would have been easier to leave it and sleep in the spare room, but I would have known the mess was still there. It would have plagued me. I had to get rid of all traces of Piers' break in.

I've already decided not to report him to the police. I can't face it. It would mean seeing him again, raking over our past. There's enough going on in my life right now, without adding to the layers of drama. It's bad enough that we still own a business together. If I didn't loathe him so much, I'd give him the whole lot, just to be rid of him. But he doesn't deserve any generosity – not after what he did, so he'll have to buy me out. I'll let my solicitor handle it.

I pass the mill house and the café on the corner, nod hello to a couple of dog walkers. Today, I decide to walk across the *quomps* – the area of reclaimed grassy marshland by the river – rather than along the path. The grass has been recently mown, and its scent draws me. It's still dewy, and dark clumps of dead grass cling to my trainers.

A couple of swans fly overhead to land on the water with a honk and an inelegant splash. Two guys in kayaks paddle past. One of them catches my eye and we share a smile at the swans' crash landing. I turn away and admire the Victorian bandstand up ahead, wondering if it's still in use. It looks like something out of a fairy tale. That would be a lovely way to spend an afternoon – a Sunday picnic on the grass listening to the band playing traditional tunes. Maybe I'll ask Jack if they still play there. I hope so. Maybe he'll ask me to go with him. Looks like someone's up there now. On the bandstand. I'm sure I didn't see them there a second ago.

I slow my pace. Catch my breath.

They're looking this way. As I draw closer I feel a familiar ringing in my ears. A rush of blood. A tightening in my chest.

No.

Not again.

She stands in the centre of the bandstand staring at me. Anger etched across her face. But this time, her anger twists into a sneer. As I draw closer, the sneer becomes a smile. Mocking. As if she's in on a secret I know nothing about. I keep on walking but I can't feel my feet beneath me, just my legs moving forward like I'm walking on air. Drifting past as though in slow motion, and all the while she follows me with her eyes. The morning light has dimmed, the smell of cut grass replaced by the damp scent of the river at night. My heart thumping in my ears, pulsing down my arms.

Time has slowed. It's me and her. And I know she means to do me harm. She hates me. I want to run and scream in terror, but I'm still moving ever-forward in slow motion, stuck in this place out of time for as long as she wants me here. I have no choice but to endure her stare until she releases me. Is she a figment of my imagination, or a memory of something I'd rather forget? I hear a sound to my right. A steady thud. A flash of crimson. I glance up and the spell is broken. It's a jogger in a cherry-red t-shirt. The sunshine has returned, the birdsong, the cry of gulls. My heart rate slows. I take in a lungful of air and turn back to look at the bandstand. But I already know it will be empty.

She's gone.

I come to a stop and glance all around me, turning three-hundred-and-sixty degrees to double check. The woman is nowhere in sight. The morning has been restored. But it's too late – my equilibrium has been disrupted. I know I'll spend the rest of the day remembering her face, her bitter smile, the feeling of encroaching darkness, the moisture-laden air, the damp scent of the river. I cast my eyes over the bandstand once more. But she's not out here, I know that now. She's in my head.

CHAPTER TWENTY THREE

I reach the rowing club in a daze. I'm sure these flashbacks, or visions or whatever the hell they are, are getting worse, becoming more frequent. The woman looks more and more real each time I see her. Like if I touched her she would be solid. Flesh and blood. Like I could speak to her and she would answer. Although, I'm not sure I'd want to hear what she had to say.

Jack is already in the boatshed. I can see him through the neat rows of shiny upturned boats on their stands. I'm wearing my baseball cap pulled down low today. I don't want him to ask about the cut on my head. If I tell him about Piers' break-in last night, it might scare him off. Nothing like a lunatic ex-boyfriend in the picture to repel any possibility of a future relationship.

So many mixed emotions course through my body. I really want to go rowing with Jack right now, but what happens if I have another hallucination while I'm out there? He'll think I'm crazy. Not to mention the fact that it's dangerous. I could capsize, and the thought of tipping into the cold, green water terrifies me. But how can I not go? I'll have to push the woman from my mind, and try not to think about falling in. I'm an experienced rower. I can do this.

'Hey, you.' Jack comes out of the boatshed, making my stomach swoop. His smile is intoxicating.

'Hi,' I say, feeling suddenly shy.

'You okay?' he asks, stretching his arms out to the side, warming up.

'Yeah. You? How was your row yesterday afternoon?'

'Good, thanks. Two of my students beat their previous times, so we celebrated in the bar afterwards. You should've come down. It was a laugh.'

I think about how I actually did spend my evening, wishing I'd known Jack was down here. I would certainly have joined him if I'd realised. Maybe I could've avoided the scene with Piers.

Too late now.

'Sounds good,' I say.

'Shall we get the boats out?' he asks. 'You warmed up?'

'Yeah,' I lie. I would've been nicely warmed up from my walk, if not for the terrifying hallucination which chilled me to the bone.

Our rowing session is a good one. I don't freak out, or capsize, or cry, or make a fool of myself in any way, which is a bonus. We get back to the boat club an hour later, my limbs aching in a good way.

'Got time for a coffee?' he asks.

'Okay.'

We clean the boats and put them away before heading upstairs to the clubhouse bar. I realise I haven't been up here since my accident. It's a huge space, ultra-modern with wide leather sofas and low coffee tables arranged artfully around the edges, interspersed with regular tables and chairs. But the most eye-catching feature is the stunning floor-to-ceiling window which runs the length of the room, and makes the most of the beautiful scenery. Even better, there's a glass door which leads out onto a vast wraparound balcony giving a bird's eye view of the river below.

'Wow,' I say. 'It's gorgeous up here.'

'Yeah. It was refurbed last year. We're lucky.' He runs a hand over the top of his head. I can't help imagining running my own hands over his hair and down the back of his neck. Him with his fingers tangled in my hair. Kissing, touching…

'Tea? Coffee?' he asks.

I flush. 'Coffee please.'

'Take a seat, I'll be back in a minute.' He strolls over to the bar, nodding to a couple of guys who are sitting on a sofa, talking loudly about race times and river conditions. Jack starts chatting to a girl who's serving the drinks. She lights up when she sees Jack, flirting shamelessly, flicking her hair and pouting. I hope I don't come across like that when I'm around him. I'll have to try and keep my feelings in check. I can't embarrass myself... again.

I don't sit down straightaway. Instead, I wait by the window and gaze down at the sparkling river, watch it meander all the way up to the sailing club and beyond. The mass of boats, like blue and white toys, their delicate masts sharp against the clear blue sky.

'Mia,' Jack calls.

I turn at the sound of my name.

'Sugar in your coffee?'

'No thanks,' I mouth. My head is hot. I long to take off my baseball cap and shake my hair out.

Jack walks over, drinks in hand. 'Shall we sit outside?' he asks.

I was hoping he'd suggest that. I need to feel a breeze on my face. He nods towards the door and I grasp the handle, push it open. We sit ourselves at the very edge of the balcony. Jack leans back in his chair and sighs with pleasure.

'Why would anyone live anywhere else?' he says. 'This place is the best.'

I nod and sip my coffee, tongue-tied. Too aware of him.

'So, Mia. What've you got planned for today?'

'I'm not sure.' I wonder if he's going to ask me out again. 'How about you?'

'This is my one and only break,' he says. 'I'm booked solid from 10 am with sessions all day.'

My stomach swoops with disappointment. But at least we're spending time together now.

'How's your memory?' he asks. 'Any better?'

'Not really. But, weirdly, I remembered a children's story,' I say with a smile. 'Not the most helpful memory in the world, but it's something.'

'Depends on the story.' He grins.

'The Three Billy Goats Gruff.'

'Hmm, maybe not. Is that the one with the troll?'

'Yeah. It came to me as I was walking across the bridge this morning.'

'Maybe it's a good thing,' he says. 'Maybe it means more memories will follow.'

'I hope so.' I love Jack's optimism.

'You look a bit distracted this morning,' he says. 'You sure you're okay?'

Should I tell him I've seen the woman again? Jack is my only friend. If I don't talk to him, there's no one else, other than my doctor. And I'm not seeing her again until next week.

'Do you remember me telling you about the ghost woman I saw?'

'The one from the graveyard?'

I nod and take another sip of coffee.

'Go on.' Jack nods encouragingly.

'I saw her again. Today.'

'While we were on the river?'

'No. Before, when I was on my way here. It shook me up a bit.'

'I'm not surprised. What was she doing?'

'It's going to sound a bit weird, but she was on the bandstand, staring at me. It was creepy as hell.'

'It sounds terrifying. Do you recognise her?'

'No.' I shake my head. 'But it's like she knows me and she wants to do me harm. She doesn't do or say anything, but the look she gives me is terrifying. Like she wants to hurt me.'

'Wow. That doesn't sound good.' He reaches across the table and takes my hand. He runs his thumb across the tops of my fingers, his touch sets the rest of my body on fire, and I have to fight to concentrate on our conversation. 'What does she look like, this woman?' he asks.

'I'm not sure. She's young, with blonde hair, slim. She looks crazy. Although… maybe it's not her who's the crazy one. Maybe it's me. Maybe I'm losing my mind.'

Jack tightens his grip on my hand and stares into my eyes. 'Of course you're not losing your mind, Mia. You went through a traumatic experience. It's obvious there'll be some fallout. I'm sure it's a symptom of your amnesia. Your mind trying to come to terms with everything. Look, after you told me about your accident, I did a little research online. It says that with amnesia, you can have false memories. So this woman is probably no one. And even if she is a real memory, she can't hurt you. She's just a hallucination. She's not real.'

All I can think of is that Jack went to the trouble of researching my condition online. I can't believe he's so thoughtful. 'Thank you,' I say. 'Not to sound soppy or anything, but I'm really lucky to have you as a friend.'

'Aw, shucks,' he says with a smile. 'But really, Mia. Try not to let the hallucinations get to you. And if she appears to you again, call me and I'll come over. You can talk to me anytime. I mean it.'

'And what about a therapist? Should I see one, do you think?'

'It's up to you. Personally, I wouldn't bother. They just want to take your money for letting you talk to them. And anyway, you can talk to me for free.' He finishes up his drink and lets go of my hand. 'I don't want to leave you now, Mia, but I have to go. My rowers will be here in a minute.'

'Of course,' I say, happy that he's reluctant to leave me. 'Sorry. I've been wittering on about my problems for ages.'

'No. I told you, you can talk to me anytime. I'm here for you, okay?'

I nod.

'Stay here. Finish your coffee. I'll give you a call later.'

'Thanks,' I say.

He smiles and heads back inside. I watch as he takes his mug back to the bar and leaves. The sun still blazes overhead, but I shiver now he's gone. Already lonely without him.

The rest of the morning passes slowly. There's no urgency about anything in my life. I can do whatever I want, whenever I want. But instead of enjoying this freedom, I feel untethered, like a balloon floating up and away, unsure if I'll finally come down to rest somewhere good, or if I'll fly too close to the sun and explode with a bang.

After showering and changing, I walk into town, browse in a bookshop, and then half-heartedly try on a few clothes in one of the high street's many boutiques. Lastly, I pick up some groceries from M&S and head home.

As I walk back through town, I have so many things I could be worrying about, but my head is filled with nothing but Jack. Of whether I'll be able to see him again tonight. Of whether he'll ring me, or call round after his coaching sessions. I should have asked him over to my place. Told him I could cook us some dinner – okay, bought us something ready-prepared and pretended I'd cooked it. But I don't think I could pluck up the courage to ask him round. Not after his rejection when we kissed.

I wish I knew how he really feels. Whether he's just being kind. Or whether he really likes me as something more. Is the split from his wife permanent? I don't know him well enough to ask. It would seem – rude, presumptuous. I'll just have to wait. See if he'll make a move. I decide not to cut through the priory today. Although it's a clear, bright day with lots of people around, I'm still spooked by the memory of the woman. Instead, I turn right and walk along the back streets.

At home, I kick off my shoes, put away the shopping, and make myself some lunch. I take my salad over to the sofa and flop down. As I eat, thoughts of my family come to mind. My sister yelling, and my mum crying. My mum hasn't even called me since last weekend. I wonder if she ever will. Did she forgive Cara? Did she let her come back home? I don't feel the urge to contact either of them. My mum doesn't seem as bad as my sister, but neither of them feels like a proper family.

My brain hurts to think about all that, so I stop. Pushing them down into the empty chasms of my mind. My mum and sister are part of the old Mia. Right now, I'm going to concentrate on the new me. On the rest of my life. I polish off the last of my salad, take a swig of water, and head downstairs to the office.

A few minutes later, I'm sitting at my desk staring at my tablet – my laptop is still at the PC repair place. I'm browsing through pages on the British Rowing website, at the section on qualifications and coaching. There are various levels of skills and courses on offer, and I'm not sure which one would suit me best. Looks like I'll have to call on Jack's expertise once again. I hope he isn't going to get sick of me.

I spend a while studying the images on the website. Happy people in their team kits, rowing on different stretches of water. But I'm beginning to feel a little sleepy, my eyes growing heavy. I think I may have to head back upstairs and take a nap. I blink and focus on the screen again, on an image of a girl on the water. She's staring out at me, her smile fixed forever. The river around her, deep and dark. I should turn it off, but I can't seem to stop looking at the water on the screen. The sky in the image appears to be darkening. It looks like the water is moving, growing choppier. It's not a video, it's a photo, so why is it moving?

My head swims. A whooshing sound envelops me, like water rushing into my ears. I grip the desk to steady myself, but it's not the desk any longer, it's the side of a boat.

It's dark. Freezing. And I try to cling on to the edge of the boat as someone loosens my fingers one by one. This person means me harm. They want to hurt me, physically. I feel hands on my back – pushing. And now I've lost my grip. I'm flailing forwards, gasping in fear. There's a sharp pain at the back of my head, blinding, throbbing. As I go under, I try to call out, but the water enters my mouth, my nose, my ears. I'm sinking, turning, falling. I thrash and spin around. The silent roar of water fills my head, and all I see is the wavery shape of someone's face peering down through the black water at me as I fall away into the thick, cold darkness.

CHAPTER TWENTY FOUR

My mouth is dry, my head pounding. My cheek pressed against the hard, wooden floor. Where am I?

The office.

I'm in my office at home. The sun streams in through the windows, warming my cheek, though my fingers are numb. Icy. I clench my fists. What happened? I must have passed out. Fallen to the floor.

I grow cold as I remember the flashback. Chills down my spine. A knot in my stomach. The deep water. The terror of sinking. The river enveloping me in its chilly grasp. Someone pushed me into the water. Someone tried to kill me!

I stay on the floor, curling into a foetal position. Trying to remember, but wishing I could forget. It was real. Someone tried to kill me. I close my eyes and try to replay the memory. To visualise the face of my attacker. But I can't. I open my eyes again and stare at the wood-grain of the floor, slide my hands between my thighs to warm them up. Blink. I'm too shocked to move. I don't know what to do. The police told me they thought it was an accident. But I know now that it was deliberate. Someone was trying to harm me. To kill me.

But I'm not dead. I'm very much alive.

I uncurl my body and sit up, slowly. My brain feels as though it's floating loose in my skull. Like I have the mother of all hangovers. A wave of nausea crawls over my scalp. I stop moving and take a steady breath. Thankfully, the sick feeling passes and I'm able to sit all the way up. As I grip the edge of the desk to lever myself to my feet, I recall my hands gripping the edge of the boat. The feeling of helplessness as my attacker pried my fingers free. Why would anyone want to kill me?

For my money?

Maybe.

But who? I can think of at least three people who don't like me. But would they hate me enough to kill me?

I need Paracetamol. My head pounds so ferociously I can barely see. I lurch out of the office, my hands moving along the walls to steady myself. Head bowed, eyes half closed. Painkillers first. Then I'll call the police.

I didn't make it to get the painkillers, or to call the police. I fell asleep before I got there. Lay down on the end of the bed and closed my eyes. Now, I awake to darkness and silence. My headache has eased to a dull throb, and I shiver, wrapping my arms around my body. Remembering.

I should stir myself and call DS Wright, but what if my memory is unreliable. Jack said people with amnesia often have false memories. Maybe the flashback isn't real. But it felt so vivid. I'm still shaking, for Christ's sake. I stagger to my feet and reach across to hit the light switch. This place feels so empty and cold. My stomach is in knots. If my memory is real, then whoever tried to kill me might still be out there. They might try again. I glance out of the window at the darkness, at the glittering lights along the river, my thoughts looping back on themselves. I can't think straight. I suddenly feel exposed standing here by the window. I check the doors to the balcony are locked, and pull the curtains closed, making sure there's no gap for anyone to see through.

Leaving the bedroom, I make my way upstairs, switching on the lights as I go. My phone's up here. My bag lies on the breakfast bar. I rummage around inside until I locate my mobile. There's only one person I want to talk to right now – Jack.

I pace the lounge, waiting for him to arrive. From the sofas at one end of the room, I walk past the dining table and reach the balcony doors at the other end, then I turn around and walk back again, chewing the skin around the edges of my nails, and trying to get my scattered thoughts into some kind of order. My bare feet sink into the carpet as I pace, my skin prickles with nerves.

Am I mad? Do I need medical help? Am I in danger? Do I need the police? I'm too anxious to call the emergency services. I'll be taken to the police station, or to the hospital. I'll be all alone. I'm sick of feeling so lonely. Scared. I need someone to be with me. Someone I trust.

When I called Jack, he answered straight away. I heard the quaver in my voice as I asked him if I could come over to his place. He told me not to worry. To sit tight. That he would come over to mine in a few minutes. That I didn't sound calm enough to drive, and it was too far and too dark for me to walk alone. So now all I can do is pace until the doorbell rings. Jack will know what to do for the best. I'll tell him what happened and he'll set my mind at ease.

The minutes slide by and still no Jack. Is he coming? Did something happen? Where is he? I brave the balcony and peer down. No car headlights coming down the lane. My teeth are chattering, I'm so cold.

'Mia! Is that you?' I'm startled by my name being called from below. I squint down through the railings.

'Jack?'

'You okay?' he calls up.

'I'm coming down,' I croak. Instantly, my shoulders relax. He's here. He's going to help me sort this out. Untangle my jumbled mind. Sieve through what's true and what's not.

I ignore the intercom, and lurch down the two flights of stairs to the ground floor, careless of the steepness of the staircase. Almost losing my footing several times. But I finally make it to the front door without mishap, wrench open the door to see a concerned-looking Jack standing there, his hands dug into the pockets of his jeans, his grey hoody zipped up against the chill night air.

'What's going on?' he says. 'You sounded scared on the phone. Are you okay? Are you hurt? Was it another hallucination?'

'Come in,' I say, taking a step back to let him through. 'I'm not hurt. Just a bit rattled. Thank you so much for coming. I'm sorry. I didn't know who else to call. You said if I needed to talk, you didn't mind. But if you're busy, don't worry. I'm sorry…'

'Hey, hey, calm down.' He pushes the door closed behind him and wraps me in his arms. Instantly, I feel calmer, safer. I take several deep breaths, in through my nose and out through my mouth, trying to get my panic under control. 'You're shivering,' he says. 'Here…' He unzips his hoody, slides it off and drapes it around my shoulders. I pull it close to my body. 'Let's go upstairs,' he says.

I slip my arms into the sleeves of his hoody, and I follow him up.

We sit on the sofas opposite one another. He's leaning forward so the distance between us isn't too great.

'Tell me what's happened, Mia?'

The images crowd me and I'm scared to put them into words. To give voice to the terror. But Jack came over to find out what's wrong, he's staring at me, waiting for me to begin, so I need to be brave and tell him.

I push my hair away from my face with both hands and hold it there for a second, cradling my skull. Then, I let go, return my hands to my lap and glance up at him. He's staring at me intently, so I begin.

'I was downstairs in the office, on my tablet, looking at rowing courses. You remember I said I wanted to start coaching?'

He nods.

'So, I saw this picture of a girl on the river, and I started to feel a bit weird, like I was going to faint.' I break eye contact with Jack and drop my gaze to my lap. 'I held onto the desk to steady myself, but then, all of a sudden it was dark, and I was outside in a boat, holding onto the side, while someone was...'

There's a long silence while Jack waits for me to compose myself. I look up at him and take a breath.

'There was someone else there. They were behind me in the boat. And they... they pushed me into the water. It felt so real. Like I was there in the cold water. Sinking. I couldn't swim back to the surface. I looked back up and I saw their face looking down at me through the water.'

'Who was it?' Jack asks. 'Was it the girl from your hallucinations?'

'I... I don't know. It was too dark. I couldn't see. But I remember feeling shocked that they had done it. Like, I couldn't believe they would try to...'

'Oh, Mia. That must have been terrifying for you.' He stands and slides in next to me, his arm coming around me. I lean my head on his shoulder, feeling a little calmer now. It helped to talk about it. To tell him.

'What should I do?' I say. 'I should call the police, shouldn't I? Tell them I've remembered something important. They dismissed it as a rowing accident before. But it wasn't an accident, was it. Someone tried to...' I can't finish the sentence. I'm shaking again.

'Shh, shh. It's okay, Mia. I'm here. You're safe.'

'Will you call them for me? Tell them what happened?'

'Of course. Of course I will. Let me make you a cup of tea first. With sugar. You're in shock, and you're cold. It'll warm you up. It'll help. Come on.' He stands up and extends his hand. I let him pull me up and follow him across to the kitchen. 'Sit here.' He pats one of the bar stools and walks into the kitchen, busying himself with the kettle.

I sit and watch him move around the kitchen, finding the mugs, the tea, the milk, the sugar. His dark t-shirt accentuates his shoulders and his strong rower's arms. I'm enjoying gazing at his body as he moves. It takes my mind off the other thing.

'Here.' He places a steaming mug of tea on the counter in front of me, and I wrap my hands around it, the heat painfully good against my chilled fingers. He comes and sits next to me. Swivels around so my knees now face his. 'Drink,' he says.

I take a sip of the scalding liquid, and grimace. 'Too sweet.'

'Good. It's meant to be sweet. You need the sugar.'

I make another face and take another sip.

'Do you think it really was a memory?' he asks. He leans forward and looks into my eyes, resting his hands on the outside of my lower thighs, just past my knees. I'm distracted by his closeness and I have to concentrate hard to make sense of his question. 'Or could it have been another hallucination,' he continues, 'like the woman you saw in the graveyard and on the bandstand? Your mind was pretty messed up after the accident. You're seeing a lot of strange stuff.'

'That's why I called you,' I say. 'I can't seem to make sense of anything on my own. I needed to talk it through with someone.'

'Did you recognise the person in the dream?'

I shake my head. 'No, I couldn't make out their features at all. I told you, I only saw them through a layer of water. It was dark.'

'Was it a man or a woman?'

'I don't know.'

'Where were you, exactly?'

'In a boat, on the river.'

'Are you sure?' He frowns. 'You were found on the beach. So how come you were on the river?'

'I… I don't know. I suppose I could have been out at sea. It was all so—'

'So which was it, the sea or the river?'

'I told you, I don't know. It was dark.' The images of the flashback crowd my mind again, my heart rate speeds up.

'What were you doing out there at night?'

'I don't know. It's only a piece of the memory, I don't know what I was doing before or after. Why are you asking all these questions?'

'What were you wearing at the time?'

'I… I don't know.'

'What was the other person wearing?'

'I don't know… Please. Please stop asking me these questions.' My head is pounding again, my stress levels through the roof. I don't know why Jack is being so… demanding.

'Are you on any medication?'

'What?'

'Have you been drinking this evening? Taken any other substances?'

'What? Jack! No, I haven't taken anything.'

He takes his hands from my legs and sits back upright. 'Sorry, Mia. I wasn't being aggressive on purpose. I was just asking you the types of questions the police will want to ask you. I'm preparing you for a long night of questioning. Do you think you're up to it? I'm worried about you.'

I can't even answer, I'm so shaken.

'Mia?'

I shake my head.

'I'm sorry,' he says, taking my hand. 'I overdid it. Forget those questions. I'll take you to the station. If you finish your tea, we can go now.'

I close my eyes for a moment. The thought of sitting in a cold police station at night, answering question after question about a scary memory, is too overwhelming.

Jack lets go of my hand and gets to his feet. 'Shall we go?'

'Do you think… Do you think it would be okay if we left it until the morning? It's just… I'm so tired. If I could just get some sleep. Then I'd be fresher. Things might seem clearer.'

'Are you sure?' he says, with a frown. 'Hopefully, they won't be as forceful as I was. But I just wanted you to know what it might be like. I'm sure they'll go easier on you.'

'… I don't know. I… Well… Okay. Maybe I should go. I guess the sooner I let them know, the sooner they can start looking into it.'

'Absolutely.'

'Let me get my coat,' I say, standing up.

'As long as you're sure it was a real memory,' he adds, 'and not another dream or hallucination. Just be prepared – they might need you to speak to a psychiatrist, or someone in the medical profession, to see if they can work out what's true and what's not.'

'Oh, yes. I suppose there's all that.' My lip trembles. 'No, no. I don't think I can handle it tonight. I'm too tired. And, you know – I guess it could have been another hallucination. The police did think it was an accident. Oh, I don't know! I just don't know.' I put my mug back on the counter and cover my face with my hands.

'I'm sorry,' he says. 'I've made things worse.'

'No, no you haven't. I feel much better now you're here.'

'Really? Well, if you're absolutely sure you don't want me to take you tonight, then let's not think about the police anymore. Come here.' He puts his arms around me and I stand and lean against his chest. Happy to be comforted for a moment. To let all my confusion and fear melt away for a few seconds while I listen to his steady heartbeat, and breathe in his scent. We stand like that for a moment, until he leads me by the hand over to the sofa.

He sits down and I sit next to him, catching my breath as he gazes into my eyes and runs a finger down my cheek. I wonder if he's going to kiss me. But instead, he stands and gently lays me down, lifts my feet so I'm lying along the length of the sofa. He tucks a cushion beneath my head, takes the woollen throw that sits decoratively on the sofa arm and drapes it over my body. Then he sits on the floor, by my head, and strokes my hair, soothing me, until I finally fall asleep.

CHAPTER TWENTY FIVE

I'm woken by the doorbell. My body stiff, my head sore, my eyes raw. I'm on the sofa in my clothes, covered by my duvet. There's a post-it note on the coffee table. I reach across to grasp it.

Hey sleepy head,
You were dead to the world, so I took off.
Hope you're feeling better this morning.
Call me if you need anything.
Jack x

Shit. The events of yesterday come flooding back. My hallucination. Jack coming over. Me, freaking out all over him. He must think I'm a basket case. Have I wrecked any chance of us being together?

Now morning's here, the vision I had doesn't seem quite as real, or quite as bad as I made out. I think I was probably overreacting. I'm pretty sure it was my mind messing with me. I mean, real memories don't feel like that, do they. Real memories are like when Jack was here last night. Like going rowing, going up to London on the train, Piers, the party – all the stuff that happened after the accident. Those all feel like actual memories. But the weird woman on the bandstand, the drowning incident last night – they felt like something else. Like I was physically present in that moment – like they were hallucinations rather than memories. It must have been my mind playing tricks. It had to be. Because the alternative…

The doorbell rings again. I throw off the duvet, run my fingers through my hair and answer the intercom at the top of the stairs.

'Hello?' I say.

'Is that Mia? Mia James?' A woman's voice.

I hesitate, and then: 'Yes, I'm Mia.'

'It's DS Emma Wright here. And DC Blackford. Can we come in?'

'Erm, yeah, sure. I'm upstairs, on the top floor. Come up.'

I'm still half-asleep, but I press the buzzer to let them in. Then I shove the duvet behind the sofa. Luckily, I'm still fully clothed from yesterday, but my mouth tastes vile. I'll have to take care not to breathe on them. I scan the room, shove Jack's note into my jeans pocket and tip my half-drunk cup of tea from last night down the sink. I don't know why I'm bothering about the state of the place. I'm sure they've seen far worse.

Footsteps on the stairs, getting closer, and then I see them. They're both dressed casually in jeans. Him in a shirt, her in a t-shirt and baseball jacket. They seem younger today, without their smart clothes. What could they want? I thought my case was closed. It's funny how they're here now, today, when I almost called them last night.

'Hi,' I say.

'Hello,' DS Wright says. 'Nice place you have here. Great views.' We all turn to look at the view at the other end of the room.

'Really draws your eye,' DC Blackford adds.

'How are you?' DS Wright asks.

'Okay,' I say, feeling anything but. 'Can I get you a cup of something?'

'Tea would be lovely,' she replies. He nods in agreement.

'Please, sit down.' I gesture to the dining table and they both sit facing the view, murmuring about the river, and the great position of these houses, while I busy myself making drinks. I check my mobile phone. No missed calls or messages. It's already quarter to ten, I must have slept for hours. I should call Jack. Apologise for dragging him over here last night.

I bring their drinks over, place them on the table. I'm too keyed up to sit down, so I stand by the breakfast bar, cradling my tea, wondering again why they're here.

DS Wright comes straight to the point. 'Mia,' she says. 'Something has come to light that leads us to believe your rowing accident may not have been an accident.'

I put my tea down on the counter top and look from DS Wright to DC Blackford. He has his notebook out, but both of them are staring at me. I remember the terror of yesterday's episode – of sinking beneath the water, of the face staring down at me. I know I dismissed it just now, but could it have actually happened?

'What,' I whisper, my voice caught in my throat. 'What's come to light? What do you know?'

'We've found a body in the river,' she says. 'The body of a woman.'

I go cold. I grope behind me, feeling around for one of the breakfast stools, which I manoeuvre myself onto. 'A body? You mean… a *dead* body?' Of course they mean a dead body. What other kinds of bodies are there? 'Who was she?' I ask.

'We haven't identified her yet,' DC Blackford answers. 'She was in the water for quite a while, so we'll have to use dental records.'

'Yes, thank you, Chris.' She shoots him a black look. 'Now, at this stage, we're not saying this discovery and your amnesia are connected. But, we do believe the body went into the water at about the same time you were washed up on the beach. And she also has a head wound.'

'So, are you saying that this body you found and my accident *could* be connected?' My mind whirrs. Could someone have tried to kill us both?

'Two independent boating accidents at the same time in the same area would seem very unlikely, so, yes, they may very well be connected.' She takes a sip of her tea. 'But we haven't found another boat to tie the deceased to a rowing accident, so it could be that the boat we found last week was one used by the deceased and not by you. It was only rigged up for one rower, so you couldn't both have been rowing. Your accident may have been non-rowing related – particularly as you were found on the beach, and not on the river. Anyway, the point is, we're pursuing all lines of enquiry.

'Have you managed to regain any of your memories? It would be extremely helpful if you could remember anything. Even the smallest, most insignificant detail could help us.'

Now is the time to tell them. With this new development, I realise I have to let them know what I… experienced.

'There is something,' I say.

DS Wright sits up straighter, and Chris' pen hovers over his pad. 'Go on,' she says.

'I was actually going to call you this morning, because yesterday I had some kind of flashback. I don't know if it was an actual memory, but it felt pretty real.' They don't interrupt me, so I continue. 'It was night time, and I was in a boat. I was gripping onto the side.' As I speak the words, I feel myself pulled back into the vision. I take a deep breath to steady myself. 'Someone was there with me. Behind me. Prising my fingers off the edge of the boat. They pushed me into the water. I had a terrible pain in my head as I went in.' I hear the rise in my voice, the tremble and quaver, but I need to keep calm. 'I felt weak, but I managed to spin myself around in the water and look up.'

'Did you see the person's face?' she asks.

'Yes, but I couldn't make out their features at all. I was looking up through the water. And it was dark.'

'Was it a man or a woman?'

'I don't know. I'm sorry. I wish I could remember more.'

'Would you come back to the station with us now? Give a full statement? Maybe something else will come back to you.'

I nod wearily. My eyes are scratchy, my body stiff and uncomfortable from sleeping on the sofa.

'We can drive you,' she says.

'Do you mind if I meet you there?' I say. 'I have a couple of errands to run, but I can be there within an hour.'

She nods. 'Let's say eleven o'clock.' She takes a few more swigs of tea and stands. DC Blackford does the same.

Good. At least that gives me a few minutes on my own. Some time to gather my thoughts before I go. I don't know whether to feel relieved or frightened at this turn of events. Could I be closer to finding out what actually happened to me?

CHAPTER TWENTY SIX

I'm exhausted. I could do with spending the day in bed, but I want to see if I can catch Jack at the rowing club. I head along the river path in a daze, the mid-morning sun occasionally peeking out from scudding white clouds. It's probably too windy to row, but he might be up at the club anyway. I hope so. I've been checking my mobile every five minutes, and he hasn't called or texted. I haven't seen him since Friday night when he came over to calm me down, and I feel weird about calling him again. I don't want to be the type of girl he thinks of as annoying, or clingy. He's already done far more for me than anyone else I know. So, my reasoning is that if I go to the club, maybe I'll just happen to bump into him, and then I can gauge from his reaction whether or not he's pleased to see me.

I spent ages at the police station yesterday. I was there by eleven, like they asked. But it was gone twelve by the time DS Wright and DC Blackford were able to see me. They conducted the interview on camera and I told them pretty much what I'd told them back at home, about being pushed into the water. But this time, the process was more drawn out, and they asked me way more questions – most of which I didn't have the answers to, because of course I don't remember anything. They couldn't – or wouldn't – tell me any more about the body they found.

By the time I got home it was mid-afternoon, and I was drained. Shattered. Too tired to eat, or cry, or even feel scared anymore. All I wanted to do was climb into bed and sleep for a thousand years.

I'm halfway to the club when I see a familiar figure up ahead walking towards me. Shit. It's my charming neighbour – the lovely Suki. Possibly my least favourite person in the world – not that I know that many people. It's too late to change course or turn around as I've already caught her eye. I suppose I could ignore her, but she's my neighbour, for God's sake. I'm not going to be rude. If she wants to blank me, then that's her prerogative.

I plaster a tight-lipped smile on my face and nod my head, but, as expected, she totally ignores me and walks on past. Stupid cow. I wonder what on earth I could have done to offend her. Surely she can't believe that I was actually trying to seduce her husband the other night. I suppose I should let her go, leave her to her low opinion of me. But she's riled me and I want to find out what her problem is. Before I can change my mind, I turn and call out.

'Suki!'

She stops, but doesn't turn around. Then, she carries on walking away from me, her usually sleek bob ruffled by the wind.

'Suki, wait!' I hurry after her. 'Suki,' I say, passing her and planting myself in her path.

She gives a long-suffering sigh. 'What is it, Mia? What do you want?' Her expression is withering, and I cringe beneath her gaze.

'I… I just want to know what I've done to offend you. Why don't you like me?'

'I just don't, okay.' She makes a move to go past me, but I put my hand on her shoulder to stop her.

'Please,' I say. 'You know I have amnesia. Just humour me. Refresh my memory.'

An elderly couple walk past, giving us a curious sideways glance. I'm tempted to stick the Vs up and tell them to mind their own business.

'Have you really lost your memory?' Suki says. 'Or is that just bullshit?'

'Why would I lie about it?' I say, amazed that she would ask such a thing. 'If you must know, it's been dreadful. I don't remember anything. Anything at all.'

'Maybe that's a good thing,' Suki says. 'Although…' She sneers and shakes her head, 'some things never change, memory or no memory.'

'What's that supposed to mean?'

'I know what you've been up to with my brother,' she says, her fists clenched like she's about to punch me.

Okay, maybe she really does have a screw loose. Now she's making random accusations.

'What are you talking about?' I say.

'You've been having an affair with my brother,' she says, her eyes boring into mine, her arms folded across her chest.

'I don't even know your brother,' I reply.

'You don't know Jack?' She lifts an eyebrow.

My stomach lurches. I try to process what she's telling me.

'I saw him coming out of your place on Friday night. His taste in women has gone way downhill.'

Jack is Suki's brother? This news stuns me. I don't know why. Maybe because Jack is so lovely and Suki is such a cow.

'You're not a very good liar, Mia. You've gone bright red.' She shakes her head. 'He and Lucy were happy until you came along.'

'What are you on about?' I say. 'Jack and I aren't together. We're just friends. I'm nothing to do with his marriage break up.'

'Really?'

'Yes, really.'

But her words disturb me. She's smirking now like she's in on some private joke. Well, chances are, she probably is. Everyone else knows more about my life than I do, and it's driving me nuts.

'Oh, fuck off, Suki. Just fuck off.' Childish, I know, but it makes me feel a bit better. Not much, though.

'With pleasure,' she says. 'I didn't want to talk to you in the first place.'

This time, she does manage to skirt around me, heading off along the river. I could run after her and try to force her to explain what she meant, but I don't trust her. She could be stirring things up for her own amusement. She's definitely got a screw loose. The best thing for it is to find Jack and ask him.

Maybe – I think hopefully – maybe, Suki was lying about Jack being her brother. But why would she do that? And, thinking about it, I realise there are quite a few similarities in their looks. The same dark hair, the same blue-green eyes. I don't know why I never noticed before.

I continue walking to the rowing club, more slowly now, my mind churning. Why is it that instead of finding the answers I need, I seem to be stumbling across more and more problems? How is it that my life is getting more complicated? And what the hell am I supposed to do about it?

CHAPTER TWENTY SEVEN

I'm sitting in the rowing club bar, strategically placed by the window so I have a clear view of both the river and the clubhouse door, my attention flickering erratically from one to the other. Every time a boat comes into view, my heart jumps. Every time the bar door opens, my stomach lurches. But it's all in vain because none of the people are Jack. I've already left a voice message and a text for him, but he hasn't got back to me yet. I didn't hint at what I wanted. Just said I needed to speak with him urgently. Maybe it's simply because he hasn't seen my messages yet – maybe he misplaced his phone, or it's run out of battery. I hope it's not because he's avoiding me after the other night. That he's had enough of me already.

I wait for over two hours in the bar, nursing various hot beverages, and feeling self-conscious as groups of friends come in, chatting and laughing, comfortable in their skin. A few people nod and smile at me, but I don't go out of my way to encourage conversation. I can't allow myself to become distracted.

My earlier run in with Suki has unnerved me, finding out Jack is her brother. It makes me look at him in a different light. I pity him, having someone like that as a sister. Maybe she's just being over-protective – worrying about his marriage break-up. Blaming me for something that wasn't my fault. I guess it would explain her dislike for me.

It's lunchtime now, and the bar is really filling up. I feel conspicuous sitting here on my own, taking up a whole table, when it's clear others want to sit and eat. So I decide to leave, disappointed but also a little relieved that I won't have to face Jack just yet. I'm not sure how to broach the subject of his sister's hostility. I abandon my cappuccino. If I drink any more of the stuff I'll get the jitters even worse than I have them already.

I leave the bar, edging my way around the growing queue of people, and slip out through the door, down the stairs, and into the blustery day, my hair whipping around my face as the autumnal wind catches it. I give a last glance around the car park and boatshed, but Jack's not here. If I knew where he lived, I could go round and knock on his door. Jack told me his place was the opposite end of town to mine, but that's all I know. Disheartened, I turn away from the club and head for home along the river path.

I suppose I could ask Suki for Jack's address, but I'm sure she'd take great delight in refusing to tell me, laughing in my face, no doubt. Maybe Matt would tell me, but I'd still run the risk of her answering the door. No. I'll simply have to be patient. Either Jack will call me back, or I'll see him at the club sometime this week.

But there's no way I'll be able to wait that long. I need to talk to him… now.

This afternoon was spent in an agony of waiting. I tried calling Jack again, but he didn't pick up. I also tried calling from my landline in case he's ignoring my mobile number, but there was still no reply. Now, I'm on the quay again, heading back to the rowing club. It's probably a waste of time. It's Sunday night – I'm sure Jack won't be there. But I have to try. I have to do something. Being in the house all afternoon was driving me nuts.

I reach the club, disappointed to see it's all locked up. The boatshed, the clubhouse, all of it. Even the car park is empty. As I sit on one of the oversized rocks, a dark melancholy grips me. What am I doing walking around trying to find a man I hardly know, who's obviously off doing other things that don't include me? I realise what a desperate, sad, pathetic, needy loser I am. I have no friends, no supportive family. Someone apparently tried to kill me. In fact, they may still be out there and want me dead. At this precise moment in time, I don't even have the energy to feel scared. In fact, if the murderer walked up to me now, I'd probably tell them to finish the job. My stomach squirms.

No. I haven't quite reached that point. Not yet.

A woman on the opposite bank throws a ball into the river for her dog, a golden retriever. He looks like he's enjoying the game. The woman laughs and puts her arm up to shield herself as he shakes his coat vigorously, droplets of bright water spraying upwards, caught by the dying rays of the evening sun. Maybe I should get myself a dog – it could be a companion and a guardian. I think I'd like that. Perhaps it would put a stop to these feelings of loneliness which randomly seize me, leaving me breathless and afraid.

I let my mind rest a while, staring at the woman and the dog, at the river, its rippling surface disturbed every now and then by passing boats. Will I ever feel settled, calm, normal? Will I ever stop being surprised by the constant revelations about my life?

I realise it's been two weeks since I was found on the beach. Two weeks of amnesia, and I feel further away than ever from the truth of who I am. Perhaps it would have been better if Piers had left me in the hospital. If I'd been forced to start from scratch with a new identity. But he didn't. I'm here, and I have to deal with it. I open my handbag and angrily root around for my phone. There's hardly any battery left. I stab at the screen, hitting the redial button. Surprise, surprise, it goes straight to voicemail.

'Jack, I've left you a couple of messages. I really need to speak to you. I bumped into my neighbour, Suki, today, and… she told me you're her brother… she doesn't like me for some reason.' I give a nervous laugh. 'Please call me back. And, Jack, there's something else – the police pulled a body out of the river. They don't think what happened to me was an accident. I really need to talk to you.' I end the call.

Paranoia is setting in. It really does feel like Jack is deliberately avoiding me. Dodging my calls and staying away from the club. But something dawns on me – maybe this is all Suki's doing. Maybe she spoke to him, warned him off me. Persuaded him that he shouldn't see me anymore. But surely he wouldn't just cut me off like that, without at least coming to explain. I try calling him once more, but it goes straight to voicemail again, so I hang up.

As the sun vanishes behind the trees, the wind suddenly drops. The woman and her dog have gone. Everything is still, the light dimming, the air cooling. I should rouse myself. Get up and go home. No one is coming here on this quiet Sunday evening.

I tear my eyes away from the eddying water and walk up the gravel slope, back onto the path, towards home. There's no one around and dusk is falling, the Victorian street lamps lighting up along the river's edge.

I pass the children's playground – deserted and forlorn. I pass the temporary wooden café – its shutters pulled down tight. Along the winding pathway, under full-leafed trees, past sleeping ducks and swans, past empty wooden benches. Past the bandstand, its eerie shape looming out of the twilight. I carry my disappointment with me, heavy in my chest and throat.

Finally, I come to the end of the river path, and cross the narrow road, pass the empty mill house and find myself at the stone bridge. Almost home. A car approaches from behind. I get to the end of the bridge and stand back, waiting for it to pass. Then I continue on. Only a few more yards to go. The car disappears around the bend, out of view, and the whole world appears deserted once more. I delve into my bag and rummage for my house keys.

As I look up, I see a figure leaning against my wall, illuminated by the porch light, dressed in jeans and a navy hoody.

It's Jack.

My mood lifts. He must have got my messages. All my worries evaporate as I wave at him. He raises his hand and smiles.

'Hey,' I say. 'Been waiting long?'

'No, I've been next door at Matt and Suki's. Saw you coming, so I thought I'd pop down and say hi.'

'Did you get my messages?' I say. We kiss on the cheek before I slot my key into the lock.

'Messages?' he says. 'No… my phone provider is so useless.'

At least that explains why he never replied.

'Coming in?' I ask, a sudden feeling of happiness enveloping me. 'I could make us something to eat if you're hungry.'

'Sure. Sounds good.' He follows me inside.

'You didn't tell me Suki was your sister,' I say as I walk into the hall and punch in the code for the alarm. 'I saw her earlier today. I don't think she likes me very much.'

'No, she doesn't,' he says, 'and neither do I.'

Before I can register my shock at his words, a thunder crack of pain explodes in my skull and I crumple to the ground.

CHAPTER TWENTY EIGHT

The splash of water. The cold night air. A tang of iron. The scent of water – loamy and thick. A pain in my head so deep it feels as though my brain has been dipped in acid. I hear my heart beating, wondering if that's a good thing, or whether silent oblivion would be preferable. Through heavy lids, I peer out, squeezing them shut once more when I see him.

Jack is here with me. Him, sitting in the boat, intent on rowing us somewhere. Me, curled up on the wet floor before him, my ankles tied with duct tape, my wrists bound behind my back, even my mouth is taped shut. I locate the source of the metallic smell – coiled around my body are thick, oily chains.

My throat is thick with fear. I try to halt the shaking which now grips my body. I don't want Jack to know I'm awake. Did he really say he didn't like me? Did he knock me out and bring me here? How long have I been unconscious? I peer up at him again. Give a muffled whimper when he catches my eye.

'So, they found Lucy,' he says, making me jump. 'I got your message. Looks like our time together is up.' His voice sounds the same as ever. How can he be so calm while he has me tied up like this? What the hell does he mean: *they found Lucy?*

My body twitches. I try to shift myself into a more comfortable position, but it's hopeless. My legs are numb. My head feels as though it's being stabbed by a thousand daggers. My right hip throbs, my arms are screaming in pain where he's bound them at an awkward angle. I try to speak… to yell at him, but all I can do is make strangled noises through the tape across my mouth. I want to ask him what he hopes to achieve by taking me captive. To know what he means by *they found Lucy*. To know if he's planning to kill me. To scream at him, call him a bastard and a wanker. But I can't.

'I honestly didn't think you'd wake up again tonight,' he says. 'I hit you pretty hard with that rock. It's a shame for you that you're not still unconscious. It would be better that way. Better for you. Less scary.'

My shaking increases. My legs are trembling so much, they're rattling the chains. My mouth is dry and my hands are so cold I can no longer feel them.

'I knew it would only be a matter of time before they found her,' he says, his voice rising and falling over the splash of the oars, his gaze fixed ahead. 'But you… You were a disappointment, turning up on the beach like that. God only knows how you survived, Mia.' He flashes me a look of hatred that makes me recoil. 'Your amnesia was a stroke of luck,' he says. 'But those flashbacks… they really had me worried. I had to keep you close, in case you remembered.' He glances down at me again, his expression softer this time. 'I know you're scared, but I can't let you go, Mia. You belong at the bottom of the ocean. It's where you should've been all along. Saved us all this hassle.'

His vile words stick to the inside of my head, fixed there like leeches to bare flesh as my heart ricochets off my ribcage. He killed his wife. He lied to me. He said they'd split up, but it's not true. I don't want to believe he did it. If Jack killed his wife, then what happened to me that night? Did I catch him in the act? Startle him? Did he turn on me next? Did he throw me in the water along with his wife, thinking me dead too? Was that *his* face I saw staring down at me in the water from the boat? How did I manage to survive?

He was playing me this whole time. Pretending to be concerned. Pretending to be my friend, when really… really, what? I edge backwards, knowing it's useless, knowing there's nowhere for me to go. But I have to at least try to get away from him. If I don't try…

'I still can't believe you made it out of the water alive,' he says. 'What are the odds? How the hell did you survive it, Mia?' He shakes his head. 'At first, I thought you were faking the amnesia. I couldn't believe you'd actually forgotten everything that happened. It was too convenient – for both of us. Too… preposterous. But the more time I spent with you, the more I realised your memories really had gone. You were following me round like a love-sick puppy. Gazing up at me with your big brown eyes. Trusting me. Thinking I was your knight in shining armour. Asking my opinion. Calling me and texting me *all the fucking time*. Thinking you might actually get me to fall in love with you. It would be hilarious… if it weren't so sick.'

He must know how much his words are wounding me. How humiliated I feel, how terrified. But he doesn't care. He isn't the person I thought he was. Maybe I dreamed him up. Maybe I invented a handsome saviour for myself, because the alternative was too sad and depressing. But I could never have guessed how wrong I'd got it. How could I have known what a monster he'd turn out to be?

'You can cry all you like, Mia,' he says. 'But it won't change my mind. You're too much of a risk. What would I do if all your memories came rushing back? If you remember everything I'll be screwed. You'll see to that.

'My sister agrees with me. Suki's not one to keep her feelings bottled up. But don't judge her too badly. I don't know what I would've done without her support. She's the only person who knows about all this. The only person I trusted enough to confide in. I knew she wouldn't judge me, so I told her everything, the pure, unvarnished truth. She was shocked – course she was – but she's been my rock. My shoulder to cry on. The only thing she can't understand is why I've let you live this long. She always thought it was far too risky. So I'm taking her advice.'

His words hit me like more blows to the head. Hearing how much he hates me, how he and his sister were in on it together.

'Anyway,' he continues, 'I'm sick of pretending. Of having to keep on seeing you. Faking concern, when all I really want to do is… is…

'So, that's why we're here,' he says, pulling harder on the blades. 'We'll finish this where it all started. We'll do it properly this time. I'm going to take you far, far out to sea. Further than last time. I'm well prepared. You might have already noticed the heavy-duty chains,' he says, inclining his head. 'Those are for you. I'm afraid there won't be any chance of swimming to shore tonight. Not this time, Mia.'

Despite the cold, I break out into a sweat at his words. I wish I could speak, so I could reassure him that I won't tell anyone what he's done – I would swear an oath of silence. But he wouldn't believe me. He doesn't care. Poor Lucy. She was married to this man. He needs to be locked up… for a long time.

I can't believe I fantasised about this guy. That I wanted us to be together. His face is set, concentrating on getting us where he wants us to be. His muscled arms pull at the blades with hardly any effort. His powerful legs slide back and forth. This isn't one of the river boats we normally use. It's wider, more spacious. I guess that's because we're going out to sea. It needs to be more stable, because of the waves. Oh my God, I'm going to die.

No one knows I'm out here. No one knows I'm in danger. The police don't even know whose body it was they found in the river. Even if, by some miracle, they have already found out and they go to Jack's house, it will be too late for me. They won't have any idea that I'm tied up on an ocean-going boat with a murdering psychopath. By the time they work out that Jack is responsible for his wife's death, I'll be dead.

And I don't want to die.

I test my bonds. There's no chance I'm getting out of these on my own. I cast my eyes about wildly, wondering if there's anything sharp nearby that I could use to cut myself free. Maybe a rough edge on one of the chain links. But I can't move, and, anyway, I'm in Jack's direct line of sight. He'll see me if I try anything. A tear escapes down my face. Salt water. The thought makes me shudder. I can't panic, I have to keep calm. *Think. Think. Think.*

I realise with horror that my bladder is full. Please don't let me humiliate myself in front of him. Now I've thought about needing the bathroom, I can't seem to focus on anything else. Another tear, and another. A stream of them merging, falling.

If I come out of this alive, I promise I won't waste another second feeling sorry for myself. I may be alone in the world, but it doesn't have to stay that way. I really don't want to die. I want to live a good, long life with someone to love, maybe start a business, or a family. Do something worthwhile. I have money. It gives me options. But why am I thinking all these things now? Why now do I appreciate my life? Now, when I don't have a cat's chance in hell of living it.

I close my eyes and try to focus again. Try to think of a plan. Maybe, when the time comes for him to… do it, maybe I could swing my legs out and kick him in the balls. But what then? Unless I can free myself, hurting him will only make him madder, more dangerous.

It's hopeless.

'Nearly there,' he says. 'It's so beautiful out here in the bay at night. The stars are so bright away from all that light pollution on land. But you've ruined it for me, Mia. How will I ever enjoy coming out here again?'

So don't kill me, I want to yell. *Turn around before it's too late. Keep your perfect memory of the bay at night. Of the stars. Don't sully the image with my murder.*

Oh God, no. He's slowing down. He's stopped rowing. We're bobbing about in the bay. He's staring at me and I'm begging him with my eyes. Pleading with him not to do this. To take pity. Have mercy. My pulse is pounding in my ears. The blood is whooshing in my head. Whirring, making me feel dizzy. It's all so surreal. This can't be happening.

Jack lets go of his blades and leans towards me, sending my fear spiralling upwards. I cringe away from him, my wet, trembling body rebelling against what's about to happen. As he grips me under my armpits, I tip my head violently trying to get close enough to head butt him, but he's wise to that, and keeps me at arm's length. There's nothing I can do, I've run out of time. No one is here to save me and he's not about to change his mind. Within seconds, he leans me backwards over the side of the boat, and I hang there, feeling like my back is about to break as he heaves up the chains.

I can't breathe properly. I can't pass out, I have to stay alert. Slow my breathing, calm down. If I want to get out of this, I need to fight back, before it's too late. I imagine I see an expression of regret flash across his face. Maybe he won't do it. But it's nothing more than a trick of the light. His face is set. Determined.

'One last mercy,' he says, ripping the tape from my mouth. 'You'll drown quicker without it.'

I'm frozen in shock. The boat tips precariously for an instant, and I think we're both going to end up going in. But, at the last moment, Jack leans back and the boat rights itself. The chains go over with a deep splash, and I'm not prepared, I'm not ready. It can't really be happening. But it is.

I manage to suck in a deep breath as I'm yanked overboard by the sinking metal, suddenly, violently. The waves smother me. I'm tugged down fast. The water invades my nose and ears. My mouth. My eyes are open, but all is black. Sadness mingles with horror. This is it. My final moments. No one will know what happened to me. No one will even care.

Down I go. How long until I hit the bottom? I try to hold on to the last bubbles of air in my lungs. Try not to be overcome by fear again, to remain lucid for my last precious seconds, staring upward at the darkness where I now see a pinprick of white. A dot of light expanding, like a never-ending tunnel stretching into the distance. A trick for the dying to make them believe they're going to a better place. Do I believe in all that?

I convulse, my body thrashes against the chains. My eyes feel like they're about to pop out of my skull, the pressure in my head is so great. There must be a pocket of air somewhere down here.

I *need* air.

Please, someone, help me.

I don't want to die.

Please.

CHAPTER TWENTY NINE

The light expands to fill my vision. My lungs are about to explode. I squeeze my eyes shut. A feeling of lightness envelopes me and then the night air hits. Cold and salty. Bright and loud. A whirring sound that deafens. Amplified, metallic voices. Movement. I'm gasping and retching. Seawater in my nose and throat, stinging my eyes as I try to draw in deep lungfuls of frigid air.

I realise I'm being carried in someone's arms, my clothes heavy and dripping. A man in a diving suit. He deposits me on the ground. Or in a boat? We're illuminated from above. I choke out mouthfuls of foul-tasting salt water. It burns the back of my throat. My chest feels as though it's on fire, but the rest of my body is cold to the marrow of my bones.

Shit! Jack tried to kill me. He threw me overboard. I thought I was dead. I felt the last few seconds of my life ebb. I felt myself sinking, drowning, dying. But now I'm here, coughing my lungs up, trying to breathe, trying to get my thoughts straight. It seems the bright light I saw from the briny depths wasn't a stairway to heaven, but a helicopter searchlight.

Have I really been rescued – or is this merely the fantasy of a dead woman?

CHAPTER THIRTY

Three Weeks Later

Autumn has come early. Cold rain cleansing away the dust of August. The wind doing its best to strip green leaves from the trees before their time. But, no matter what the weather does, every day I go outside and I run. I run to remember and I run to forget.

Today, my feet pound the pavement away from the river, heading instead along busy main roads choked with cars and ugly out-of-town office buildings and superstores. I can't even look at that pretty stretch of water anymore without feeling sick and panicky. Until I leave this town, I don't think I'll ever be able to live a proper life. Christchurch has been tainted for me. Which is why I'm selling my house.

Even now, as I run in the rain, the estate agent is back at the house with a wealthy couple from London. It's their second viewing – they want it as a holiday home – and the agents are confident they're going to put in an offer today. Houses like mine are in great demand, apparently.

As for me, I want to live in a much larger town than Christchurch. A place where I can be anonymous for a while until I recover from the trauma of the past few weeks. So, I'm moving to Cheltenham in Gloucestershire. I've put in an offer on a beautiful Georgian mansion house in the town centre. No rivers or oceans in sight. I'll be happy if I never have to get into a boat again.

That night, when Jack tried to kill me, feels like months ago. I can't believe it's been just a few weeks. Yet, at the same time, it only seems like yesterday. The fear and despair I felt are so fresh and raw.

It was my neighbour, Suki's husband, Matt Willis, who saved me. He glanced out of the window that night and saw "someone" bundle my unconscious body out through the back gate. He was about to call the police when Suki tried to stop him. They argued, but eventually she broke down and told him a version of events where she believed I deserved to die.

Thankfully for me, he called the police anyway, explaining that Jack was planning to kill me. They mobilised police boats and a helicopter. Two officers dived down after me. They managed to free me from the chains, and haul me out of the sea. If they had arrived just thirty seconds later, I would have been dead. They saved me. Just in time.

The rest of that night was a blur. I remember being wrapped in some kind of huge metallic blanket. Then, I must have passed out, because I woke up in a hospital bed.

A day or so later, I remember DS Wright visiting me in hospital, asking me if I had anyone who could stay with me for a while. A member of my family, or a friend who would look after me and make sure I was okay. I remember how she took my hand in hers, a surprisingly intimate gesture for a police officer. I must have been semi-delirious, for the first name that came into my mind was *Jack*.

Suki was arrested for being an accessory to attempted murder. Jack was arrested for the murder of his wife, as well as my attempted murder. Of course, he's denying it. Saying it's all my fault. That I drove him to it. He's even trying to pin his wife's murder on me. But the police have formally charged Jack and Suki, and they're now both locked up, awaiting trial.

My mobile phone buzzes in my jacket pocket. It could be the estate agent with news, so I slow my pace a little and pull out my phone. It's an unknown number and I debate whether or not to answer it, but I guess it could be important, so I slide my thumb across the screen to accept the call.

'Miss James?'

'Speaking.'

'It's Mike Frenchay here, from The PC Repair Shop.'

'Sorry, who?'

'You left your laptop with us a few weeks ago. You wanted us to try and recover some emails for you.'

'Oh, yes.' I remember now. Something to do with Piers deleting my messages. I'd wondered if there was something Piers didn't want me to see about our business arrangements. All that seems unimportant now.

'Sorry it's taken so long,' he continues, 'but I've managed to retrieve some of the more recent emails for you. We're open till five if you want to pop over now?'

I check the time – four twenty. The shop is on my way back so I may as well call in there today. 'That's great,' I reply. 'I'll be there in about ten minutes.'

'Okay. See you in a while.'

I slip my phone back into my pocket. The rain is heavier now. The wind driving into my back. The PC shop is back the other way, so I turn around and face the full force of the weather, squinting and lowering my head to protect my face from the needles of rain. The most I can manage is a jog. No one else is foolish enough to be walking or running in this weather. Instead, rows and rows of cars stream past, headlamps on, windscreen wipers set to turbo mode.

Ten minutes later, I push open the door to the little store. The bell jangles above my head. The PC guy looks up from the counter. I push down my hood and take a breath. I'm dripping all over the shop floor.

'Nice day for a swim,' the guy says.

I smile and roll my eyes at the weather. 'It's lashing down out there.'

'You walked?'

'Can't you tell?'

We give polite chuckles. I tell him who I am and he slides my laptop out from under the desk, along with some paperwork.

'Wait a moment,' he says. He turns and goes through the door which leads to the back. A few seconds later he returns. 'Here,' he says, passing me a towel over the counter.

'Thank you so much.' I wipe my hands and face and place the towel next to my laptop, thinking what a nice guy he is.

'You're not planning on walking home are you?' he says. 'Even with a bag, your machine will get wet in this weather. It's chucking it down out there.'

I hadn't thought about that.

'Shall I call you a cab home?' he asks.

'That would be brilliant. Thank you.'

He pulls his phone from his pocket and calls me a cab, reading out my address from the invoice next to my laptop. 'Should be here in about ten minutes.'

'You're an angel,' I say.

'All part of the service.' He smiles. 'Now, about these emails. Like I said, I couldn't get them all, but I managed to retrieve some of the more recent ones. Here…' He opens the machine and shows me my inbox and sent folder. 'Most of August's emails are there, and a few from July.'

'Thank you. That's great. How much do I owe you?'

Luckily I have my bank card and some spare change on me, so I settle up and wait for my cab to arrive. He gives me a plastic bag to shield my laptop from the weather. We make a little small talk and then he's called away by a phone ringing in the back. While I'm waiting for my cab, I decide to take a quick peek at some of the emails he retrieved for me.

Most of it's spam. I'm specifically looking for messages from Piers – to see if there's anything dodgy about our business that he might have deleted after the accident. But it's all innocuous stuff – nothing that's worth hiding or deleting. Then my eyes alight on a message sent from the rowing club on the day before my original accident, back in August. It's marked as unread, but the subject heading reads:

What the fuck

I click on it. My eyes skim to the bottom of the email to see who it's from.

It's from Jack.

As I read Jack's message, a sick feeling sweeps across my body. The words swim before my eyes, wavering and reforming. Blurred and then suddenly sharp. I reread the email with a crawling sensation in my belly.

The PC guy returns from the back room. He starts speaking to me, but I'm not listening. My body feels suddenly heavy, my head suddenly too full of memories. They crowd my mind, jostling for space. Throwing up new and more terrible glimpses into the real me. And I wish with all my heart that I could go back to forgetting. That my mind could remain a deep void of nothingness. Wiped clean. Innocent.

I sink down onto the floor, knocking the laptop onto the tiles with a dull crack.

'Are you okay?' The PC man rushes out from behind the counter. Crouches in front of me as I lie there, curling my knees into my body. Wishing I could shrivel up and die. Wishing I could disappear. Wishing I was lying dead at the bottom of the sea.

CHAPTER THIRTY ONE

Five weeks earlier

Right on time, her Fiat pulls into the car park. I'm sitting on one of the large decorative rocks, waiting. It's that secret silent time between night and morning when only creatures are awake. Way after sunset, but not close enough to dawn. Dark and cold. Nothing stirring. The half-moon casts just enough light to see by. My heart starts to race. I should've done this a long time ago. I'm doing her a favour really. She needs to know. I called her earlier today to tell her to meet me here. To tell her that I have some information about her husband. She sounded annoyed. Said she was busy all day. That they were going to a party this evening. So I told her, okay, come after the party. How about 2 am? Surely she wouldn't be busy then.

'Don't be ridiculous,' she said. 'I'm not meeting you at two in the morning.'

'Come, or don't come,' I said, 'but I think you'll want to hear what I have to say.'

I wasn't sure if she would show. But here she is. She couldn't resist. No going back now.

I haven't been sitting here long. I spent the past ten minutes getting one of the boats out. It's now on the shingle by the water's edge waiting for me. I'm going to head out on the river afterwards. It's one of my favourite things to do – to row at night when everyone's asleep. Makes me feel like I'm the only person alive. The moon reflecting off the water. The stars winking down at me. I told Jack about my secret night-time trips down the river. Asked if he wanted to join me. That's when it all started between us – one cold, clear March night. A night that changed my life.

I finished things with Piers earlier tonight. He wasn't happy. At all. Stomped off to his party after swearing and shouting at me. Calling me all sorts of names. I took all the abuse and then told him goodnight. At last, I'm finally free of him. It was painful pretending to love him, when my heart lies with Jack. Anyway, I'm pretty sure Piers was only with me for my money. God knows why I went into business with him. That was a bad decision on my part. Jack is nothing like Piers. He's not materialistic at all. All he wants is to be on the water... like me.

I've been seeing Jack Harrington for almost six months. It's been wonderful. Intense. We're in love. He hasn't said the actual words yet, but I can tell. We light up around each other. He doesn't act like that around his wife. With Lucy. They barely interact at all when they're out together. She's dull, boring. From what Jack's said, they stayed together out of habit, duty, and some kind of misguided loyalty. The kindest thing is for her to know the truth. Jack is too scared of hurting her. He wants to wait for the right time. But I've told him, there is no right time in these situations. You just have to do it, like ripping off a plaster, as the cliché goes. It's kinder in the long run. So, I've decided, if he won't tell her, then I'm going to do it. Tonight. Or rather, in the early hours of the morning. Now.

She's getting out of the car, walking towards me, her blonde hair shining in the moonlight. A scowl on her face. She's always been friendly towards me, so it's a bit of a shock to see such a grim expression on her face. I stand up and move a few paces away from the car park, down the path closer to the river. I hear her footsteps behind me, following. I experience a rush of power, a fluttering in my stomach. I'm really going to do this.

I stop on the shingle bank and turn around to face her again. She's older than me by a few years. Jack said she's nearly thirty, but she doesn't look it. Tonight, she seems younger than me, if anything. Slight and slender, vulnerable, like you could snap her in two. I almost feel sorry for her. She's about to have her world turned upside down. She continues walking towards me, her scowl deepening, her eyes narrowing, her lip curling. Almost as if she hates me. It unnerves me a little, seeing such a violent expression appear on her face. But as she comes closer, I see that it must have been a trick of the moonlight. Her face is neutral.

'What's this about, Mia?' Her voice is strong, firm. She stands before me, shivering slightly in a short summer dress and sandals. Her make-up has that end-of-the-night, slightly smudged look about it, but that doesn't detract from her prettiness.

Now she's here, the carefully worded sentences I'd constructed in my head earlier desert me. Her eyes are fixed on mine, waiting. A cool breeze blows off the water, making me shiver too.

'It's about Jack,' I say.

'Obviously,' she says. 'You told me that already. Get on with it, then.'

I'm taken aback by her increasingly brusque tone, but I don't let it deter me. 'There's no easy way to say this,' I begin, 'so I'll just say it… Jack and I are in love.' I take a deep breath. 'We've been seeing each other for a while now, and he wants to be with me. I'm sorry, Lucy.' My heart is pounding. Saying the words makes me feel so liberated. I want to smile, but that would look too insensitive. I bite my lip instead.

To my surprise, Lucy smiles and shakes her head. 'Poor Mia,' she says.

'Maybe you didn't hear me properly,' I say.

'No, I heard you perfectly. You were telling me how you're in love with Jack and that he wants to be with you.'

I don't understand her reaction. Why is she taking this so well? Maybe she doesn't love him anymore… But there's a smugness about her that's making me uncomfortable. That's making the blood rush to my head. Making me uneasy.

'The thing is, Mia…' She places a heavy emphasis on my name. 'The thing is, that when you called me earlier, I was confused. I didn't know what on earth you could possibly be going to tell me about my husband that I didn't already know. So, do you know what I did? I asked him. I said: "Jack, Mia wants to talk to me about you. What could Mia possibly have to say to me about *you*?" And, do you know what he said?' She doesn't give me any time to reply. 'No? Okay, I'll tell you. He broke down and confessed everything. He told me all about your sad, seedy little affair.'

I hadn't expected this.

'So… then, you already know,' I say. 'I'm sorry, Lucy. It wasn't anything you did. Sometimes these things happen. It was out of our control. We fell in love.'

I must admit it's a relief that he actually told her. That I don't have to go into detail about it. But something's not quite right. She's smiling broadly now. My discomfort returns.

'You poor, pathetic cow,' she says. 'You might be in love with Jack, but I'm afraid he doesn't love *you*. He was distraught earlier. Begging me to forgive him. Said you were a stupid mistake. Said you meant nothing to him. Nothing at all.'

'You're lying,' I say, shaking my head, trying to quell the sick feeling that's rising in my gut. 'Just trying to make yourself feel better. Trying to discredit what Jack and I have together. I can understand that.'

'If you weren't such a man-stealing whore, I could almost feel sorry for you,' she says. Her tone is steely now. There's no trace of the quiet blonde wife I'd always seen before. She has to be lying. It can't be true. Jack is always telling me how he and Lucy are bored with each other. How refreshing I am. How funny and wild and exciting. And how the sex is incredible. He wouldn't give me up just like that. He couldn't. But I look at Lucy's face in the moonlight and she's smirking at me, a look of absolute triumph. She's enjoying her revelation. Enjoying seeing me process her devastating information. It was supposed to be *me* enjoying *my* revelation. I was supposed to be the one seeing a look of shocked disbelief on *her* face. I was prepared to witness her anger, or preferably her tears. And then I would have consoled her. Told her that Jack was still fond of her, of course he was. But now he was with me.

Instead, my features are twisted in shock. My chest hollow. I want to believe she's lying. But I know deep down that she's telling the truth. I can see it in the glitter of her eyes.

What should I do now? Should I go and confront Jack? But what if he rejects me? If he truly loved me, surely he would have left Lucy already. They have no children together. No commitments other than their house. It would have been easy to leave her. But he hasn't.

My plans for a happy ever after with the man of my dreams are ruined. Destroyed by this smug-faced little bitch. A surge of rage wells up inside me. Fury that she is causing me such absolute heartbreak. Jack is the love of my life. My soulmate – I'm sure of it. Lucy is nothing.

I growl in frustration and she laughs at me. She actually laughs out loud. I snarl and lunge forward, my hands grasping for her throat, knocking her back, desperate to put a stop to her mocking laughter. Her eyes widen and her mouth forms an 'o'. *Not laughing anymore, are you?* I tumble with her onto the footpath. As she goes down, the side of her head hits one of the oversized rocks alongside the path. I hear a cracking sound, but I don't register it properly. I'm too caught up in my rage.

I fall on top of her, the air knocked from my lungs. But I'm not winded enough to stop what I'm doing. Not breathless enough to stop the squeeze of my fingers. I lift my head a fraction so I can see her face. I want to enjoy the fear in her eyes. To revel in the knowledge that I now have the upper hand. That I hold her life in my hands – literally. So she better not bloody well laugh at me again. But instead of fear, her eyes are wide open in shock. Blank shock.

She looks… dead.

But how can that be? I hadn't wanted to kill her… had I? I simply needed to wipe the smile from her face. Anyone else would have done the same. If she hadn't been so smug, I would never have… Never… I can't believe she's actually…

It can't be true. I scramble to my feet, my pulse racing, bile in my throat, my breath ragged. Shit. What have I done? I remember her hitting her head on the rock. That must have been what… killed her. I glance around. Then I drop to my knees again, lean over her inert body. She's pretending, surely. Doing it to shake me up. To punish me.

'Lucy,' I hiss. 'Get up. Lucy, please. Stop pissing about. Get up.' I tug at her arm. Try to haul her upright. But she's limp, her head lolling to the side like a doll. I let her drop back down to the ground. She really is dead. I panic. What the fuck am I supposed to do now? Think, Mia. Think. I tap my head with my fingers, trying not to let hysteria take over. I could make it look like an accident. Yes, yes, yes, that would work. A rowing accident.

I glance up again to check that no one is around. My stomach clenches as I spy a figure up ahead, beyond the car park, heading this way.

It's Jack.

CHAPTER THIRTY TWO

What can I do? How can I explain this to him? He won't believe me. Usually, my heart lifts when I see him, but not this time. No. This time, my heart is sinking into the concrete path, puddling around my feet. He's coming closer. What am I going to say to him? He jogs across the car park toward me. Lucy lies on the ground beside the boulder, partially obscured from his view. Why has Jack come? If only he'd stayed away I could have sorted this out myself. Now he's here, I'll have to think quickly. But what can I possibly say that will sound convincing?

'Mia,' he hisses across the car park. 'Is Lucy here yet? Her car's here. What the hell did you think you were doing, calling her up like that!'

He's almost here and my mind has gone blank. I don't know what I'm going to say to him.

Suddenly, he stops abruptly. He's seen her.

'Is that… Lucy?' As if in slow-motion, he raises his eyes to meet mine. Normally a vivid aqua, they almost appear black in this pre-dawn light.

'Mia… Mia! What have you done? Is she okay? What's she… Lucy!'

'Jack,' I croak. 'It's not what it looks like. It was an accident.'

'Is she okay? Have you called an ambulance?' He rushes around the side of the rock and crouches down in front of her. 'Lucy! He puts a hand to her cheek. Lifts her wrist to check her pulse. But it's no good. I know it's too late. 'What have you done?' He twists back to me with a look of such despair that it makes me catch my breath. 'Lucy, Lucy. No!' He's turned back to her now, gathering her limp body to his chest and kissing her blonde hair. 'I'm sorry, baby,' he moans. 'I'm so, so sorry.'

I don't know what to do. What to say. I just stand here watching him. Watching my plans come to nothing. Watching the man I love cry tears over another woman.

He sobs over her body for what seems like forever. I don't know what to do. Should I comfort him? Put my arms around him. Should I cry, too?

'You killed her,' he cries. 'You killed Lucy!' He lays her back down on the ground and rises to his feet. Takes a step towards me. 'You murdered my wife, you psycho bitch!' His face is streaked with tears. His expression taut, drawn, like a beast about to tear apart its prey.

'It… it was an accident,' I stutter, leaning back.

'You meant to hurt her, though, didn't you, Mia.' He grabs my arms. Squeezes. 'She told me… She told me you called her and asked to meet. Why would you do that? Making trouble. Why did you want to speak to my wife?'

'You're hurting me. I only came here to—'

'To what?' He lets my arms go, his hands now hanging by his sides.

'You said you were going to leave her.' I hear the whine in my voice. 'But you never did. I thought if I told her about us… I thought she might kick you out and we would finally have a chance to be together properly. It's what we always dreamed about.'

He's looking at the ground, shaking his head, mumbling to himself. He raises his eyes to look at me. 'I never dreamed about it, Mia. That was your idea, not mine. And it still doesn't explain why she's lying on the ground, dead. Mia. I can't believe this. What did you do? What happened?'

'That's what I'm trying to tell you – it was an accident. A terrible accident.'

'You keep saying that. But how…' He reaches into his shorts pocket and pulls out his phone. 'You can explain it to the police. I can't even look at you anymore. They can deal with you now.'

'No,' I say, scrambling through my brain for something to say that will make him change his mind. 'Lucy… she was laughing at me. She said you told her about you and me. She said you would never leave her. Is that true?'

'Of course I wasn't going to leave my wife! But who cares about any of that now. She's… What we did was wrong, Mia. I was married. I loved her. I messed up. And now she's gone.'

His words twist into my gut. How can he dismiss our relationship so easily? 'But you said you were going to leave her. That we would be together.'

He shakes his head. 'I would never leave Lucy for someone like *you*. Someone so shallow and caught up in herself. I was weak.' He spits out the words, like poison into my ears. 'And now this. We never should have been together. You were a mistake, an awful mistake. And now she's gone.' Tears still roll down his cheeks.

I feel like I'm in a nightmare. My hands are shaking, my whole body is numb. I begin to cry, too. I'm not weeping for the girl I've just killed, I'm weeping for the look in Jack's eyes. His grief for Lucy and his hatred for me.

'But I love you, Jack,' I cry. I know my words are useless, but I can't stop them spilling out of my mouth, trying to undo some of the damage, needing to make him feel what I'm feeling. 'I know you love me too. It's just the shock making you say those things.'

'I never loved you.' He grabs my upper arm with his left hand and shakes me viciously, his fingers digging into my flesh. 'I hate you!'

I barely register the pain in my arm. It's nothing compared to the tearing grief ripping my insides apart. I've never experienced such hurt. Have I lost him forever? He lets go, a disgusted expression on his face, like I'm dirt, filth. Like I'm nothing, and he turns away, his head bowed over his phone.

'She fell backwards,' I sob. 'It was an accident. She hit her head.' But he's not even listening. He's staring at his phone. He's going to call the police and have me arrested.

I can't let that happen.

'What are you even doing here, Jack?' I'm trying to distract him. I need a minute to think. 'Why did you come down here? Was it to sort things out? To back me up?'

'You're deluded!' he says. 'When Lucy told me you wanted to speak to her, I was horrified. She wanted to confront you on her own. She said it would be better this way. But I was worried about her so I came looking. And I was right to be worried. But now it's too late. I should never have let her come here by herself.' Jack wipes at his eyes and blinks, staring at his phone, his fingers hovering over the screen. He takes a deep breath. 'We need to call the police. Now.'

It's too bad Jack's so insistent on calling the police. I've come up with a story, and I don't want to do this, but he's leaving me with no option:

'I'll tell them you did it,' I say. 'If you call them, I'll say I saw you push your wife. That I rushed over to help her and you became even more aggressive.'

He stops what he's doing and stares at me in disbelief, his expression turning to hatred and anger once again. I never thought I'd ever see him look at me that way. It's like a punch to the gut. Will he ever show me his loving smile again? The one that makes my body melt. I feel such an aching sense of loss. As though my insides have been scraped out. But, as much as I love him, I won't let him destroy my life. If I'm going to be arrested, I'll take him down with me. I must pull myself together and make him understand that I won't let him ruin my life.

'They'd never believe you.' Jack grits his teeth.

'Really? Do you want to risk it? Because don't they always suspect the husband in these situations? I'm pretty sure they'll believe me over you – the "violent" husband.' I mime air-quotes. 'I'll explain to the police how Lucy was my friend. How I called her earlier to check up on her, because she'd been confiding in me about you, about how scared she was of you. That she thought you were going to hurt her. How she asked me to meet her down here to plan her escape from you.'

'That's ridiculous. They won't believe that.'

'Are you sure?' I ask. 'It'll be your word against mine.'

'No! You can't…' He pulls at his hair, his face screwed up in disgust. 'You're twisted. I don't know what I ever saw in you. How can you lie like that? How can you…'

'Because I'm not going to prison for something that was an accident. And anyway, it's as much your fault as mine. If you hadn't cheated on your wife. Or if you'd left her like you promised, none of this would have happened.'

'So this is *my* fault? I wasn't even here! You're delusional, Mia. A total nutjob. How could I not have seen that before?' He shakes his head and then lunges at me, dropping his phone and grabbing me by the neck of my t-shirt. His other hand is curled into a fist, raised, ready to punch me.

I cringe backwards, but I manage to stutter: 'Go on, Jack, hit me. It'll only make my story more convincing.'

He glowers at me, eyes narrowed, teeth bared like an animal. But he gradually releases his grip on me and lowers his fist. Then he tears his gaze from mine and bends to retrieve his mobile.

'Put the phone away, Jack.' I say, trying to steady my voice.

He's shaking his head, but he isn't making the call. I think he'll see it my way. Otherwise, he risks being arrested for murder. I need to get my shit together. We can do this. And then, when he's calmer, later, he'll see that we had a good thing, that we really are perfect for each other. This will bond us, connect us again. When everything has settled down, we can be together once more, this time without Lucy in the picture. I have this perfect vision of Jack and me – married, with children, growing old together.

But first… first, we have to get through tonight.

A plan is forming in my mind. Of how we can do this and have everything turn out okay. I think… I think this whole episode might have been fate. A way for me and Jack to finally be together properly without all the need for secrecy and sneaking around.

'You're going to help me get rid of her body,' I say. 'We'll make it look like an accident. That she capsized and drowned. Okay?'

'What! What are you planning to do, Mia?' he says. 'You can't just dump her in the river. You can't! That's my wife. You can't do that.'

'No, she's got a head injury. We need to row out to the rocks near the harbour mouth. Make it look like she had an accident out there.'

'You can't seriously expect me to—'

'The river boats are too unstable,' I continue. 'We'll need a sea boat to get her out there.'

'I won't do it. It's monstrous. What you're suggesting is—'

'It's either that, or you're going to prison for a very long time,' I say. 'And we need to act quickly, before the sun comes up and the whole world descends on the quay for the day.'

To my relief, he slips his phone back into his pocket. I may need to get that off him, in case he changes his mind.

We spend the next ten minutes hauling a coastal four-seater out of the boat shed and setting it down on the shingle. We don't speak. Jack shoots me filthy looks, but I ignore them. This is a shock for both of us, but we have to be practical. There's nothing we can do to save Lucy, but why should we both suffer because she died? No. We need to dispose of her body, and then we can go back to getting on with our lives.

I stride back up to the edge of the car park. 'Help me put her in the boat,' I say, bending down towards Lucy's body.

'Get away from her,' he growls.

'Fine. You put her in the boat then.' I forgive him his temper – this is a shock. A stressful situation.

He turns and squats by her side, dropping his head in his hands.

'Quickly,' I say. 'If someone comes along we're screwed.'

'For God's sake, she's my wife. Give me a minute.' Finally, after what seems like an age, he scoops Lucy's body up in his arms and stands. It hurts me to see the tender look he gives her, the kiss he places on her forehead, the tears still flowing freely down his cheeks. My heart twists with jealousy as I realise he may actually have loved her.

'Put her in the boat,' I say, wanting him to relinquish his hold on her. To stop gazing at her. I want this over. I want her at the bottom of the river.

He does as I ask, hardening his features and staggering down to the river's edge. I follow him. Watch as he lays Lucy in the stern of the boat, her body curled around itself on the boat floor, her blonde hair splayed across her face, a smear of blood from the back of her head stark across the white fibreglass.

'Now, take her sandals off and throw them on the bank. You can take them home with you, later.'

He slips her sandals off her pale feet and places them carefully on the shingle.

'We'll have to bring the river boat with us, too. It has to look like an accident. Like she went out on her own and capsized.'

I jog back up to the boatshed, find a length of rope and grab a set of blades. I stride back towards the river to see Jack just standing there, staring down at his wife's body, fresh tears dripping down onto her lifeless form. We don't have time for this.

'You need to get a pair of blades,' I say. 'And another pair... for Lucy.'

He scowls and walks back up to the boatshed, shoulders hunched. At least he's doing as I ask. He's not arguing anymore. I glance around to make sure no one's coming. To check nobody's lurking in the shadows, watching us.

The boatshed is all locked up. We're finally on the water, in the coastal, towing the single behind us. I'm at the bow, and Jack's in front of me, with Lucy at his feet. It's like a bad dream. I may have had the idea to dispose of Lucy's body, but that doesn't mean I want to do this. I didn't want her to die. I feel like I'm outside of my body, looking down at us from above. At me and Jack and Lucy. At the boat we're towing behind us, bobbing on the water like a white coffin.

Jack and I don't say a word. I have so many thoughts whirling around my head, but I don't know how to articulate them. Thoughts about "us", about what's going to happen to me and Jack after today. About how we can get back to where we used to be. I know Jack will only get angry if I mention those things now, so I'm better off keeping my thoughts to myself, until afterwards. I have a horrible feeling that he won't want to see me again after this. We started our relationship out on the river at night. Now, here we are again, out on the river at night. But there's no soft laughter, no illicit kisses. I can't let this be the end. I can't.

The river is calm, and the exertion of rowing has warmed me up. I don't know how long we've been out here, but I turn my head to see we're suddenly approaching the harbour mouth, the dark expanse of the bay stretching out to the darker horizon beyond.

'We're here,' I say.

A few minutes later, we're coming alongside a bank of rocks just past Mudeford Quay.

'I can't do this, Mia,' he cries. 'Please. Don't make me do this. It's not too late to go to the police. To tell them it was an accident. If we tell them what really happened it might be okay. But this – putting her body into the water – it feels so wrong.' He turns back to look at me, his eyes beseeching.

'We're not calling the police,' I say. I have to be firm with him. Make him understand that what we're doing is for the best. 'This is between me and you. No one else has to get involved.'

'What about Lucy's parents? Our friends? What will we say to them?'

'We won't say anything. She'll have gone missing. It will all have been just a tragic accident. Which is the truth anyway.'

'Is it, Mia?' His eyes narrow. 'Is it the truth? Did she really just happen to fall and hit her head, because it seems very unlikely to me.'

'What are you saying, Jack?' I stare back at him. 'It sounds like you're accusing me of something.' An image of Lucy's face flashes into my mind, of her shocked expression as I lunged at her. But I push the memory away. I wasn't trying to kill her. I just wanted to… I don't know what I wanted – to wipe the smug expression from her face. 'This is as much a shock for me as it is for you,' I continue. 'For her to die like that… it's unthinkable.'

He turns away, his head bowed. Our boat sways in the water, our blades keeping us from scraping against the jagged black rocks.

'If we leave her here,' I say, 'it will look like she capsized, hit her head on the rocks and was swept away. I'll untie the single, if you keep our boat steady.'

My fingers shake as I loosen the knot. It takes me a while, but I finally work it free and haul the boat around so it's alongside us.

'You'll have to lift her into the water, Jack. I can't manage it from back here.'

'I don't want to do this. It's not right.'

'She loved to row, right?' I say.

'Yes.'

'So, to be in the river is a good thing. It's like… how people scatter ashes in the deceased's favourite place.'

'It's fucking nothing like that,' he says through gritted teeth. 'I'm not a child, Mia. You can't make me feel better about this. We're disposing of my wife's body at night in a river. There's nothing "good" about it.'

'I'm sorry. I'm just trying to—'

'Well don't. Just shut the fuck up and let me do this in my own time.'

I take a breath. He's scared and tired and upset. I'll give him time to compose himself. I can hear him murmuring, but I can't make out what he's saying. He's speaking to his wife's dead body. I catch the words 'sorry' and 'I love you' and other endearments I'd rather not hear. Finally, he lifts her body up and over the side of our boat, making us rock and then tip precariously to one side. I put my weight on the opposite side to balance us.

She's in the water and Jack is sobbing. Her body is just floating there, face up, unmoving. Her eyes are closed. She looks like she's asleep. Her face white, her hair floating like a golden halo in the moonlight. I untie the other knot to the boat and let it go, shoving it away from us. It's instantly taken by the current.

'You need to push her body away,' I say.

'I can't,' Jack says, his face stricken. 'You'll have to do it. I can't look at her like that. She doesn't look like my Lucy anymore.'

'Of course,' I reply. 'Of course I'll do it. You sit back in the boat and look away if it's easier.' I lean over as he sits back. I reach down over the side of the boat. She just needs a good, hard shove, and she'll be taken by the current, like her boat.

My hands enter the frigid water and I push Lucy as hard as I can. As I do so, I feel a blinding flash of pain at the back of my head. *What?* I slide my freezing, wet hands out of the water and bring them up to check my head. I'm dizzy. What just happened? I grab onto the side of the coastal to steady myself.

It's Jack! I twist around, ready to push him away. But it's too late. The end of the blade comes down on my head for a second time. His hands peel my frozen fingers from the edge of the boat and he shoves me into the water. How can he do this to me? I was doing this for us… so we could be together. I love him. The water rushes around my body, fills my nose, my ears, it blurs my eyes. I spin around and gaze up through the dark layers of water, see his wavery features peering down. See the end of the oar smash through the surface of the water towards me. I flinch backwards as shock and sorrow grip my heart. Jack is attacking me!

I want to plead with him. Make him understand. Make him love me again. But he won't listen. Not now. He's too shocked. Too angry. I have to get away from him. Make him believe I'm unconscious. That I've drowned. I must hold my breath a little longer.

So, I dive down and swim away from him.

Down into the black nothingness.

CHAPTER THIRTY THREE

Seven months later

It's bone chilling weather. Too cold even to snow. The walk from the bus stop is taking longer than I'd anticipated, and my thick woollen coat is no prevention against today's icy grip. The city is bleak and grey. Still and strangely quiet. As I stride along Thamesmead beneath leafless trees, I can smell the damp river, even though I can't see it from here. I haven't been back to London since I last visited my mum and sister, before my memories returned. I won't be visiting them today, or anytime soon.

I'm here, at last. It's a relief to get in out of the cold. They said I had to allow thirty minutes for all the security checks. I pass through the various sets of gates, steel doors and metal detectors in a daze, along with all the other visitors, showing my two forms of ID. Next, I submit to being fingerprinted, having my photograph taken and my hand stamped.

This place isn't how I thought it would be. From the outside, it looks more like a modern art gallery. But I guess this is just the visitor's section. I can't imagine the actual cellblocks are quite as sanitised and pretty. Not in a category-A, maximum-security prison like Belmarsh. It's not what I wanted for him. Not at all. But what choice did he give me?

I wasn't sure he'd even allow me to visit. I sent my request in a few weeks ago, not hopeful of hearing anything back. So it was a shock when the visiting order finally came through. But then, I guess he doesn't get too many people wanting to visit. Not after everyone found out what he did – murdering Lucy, and then attempting to kill me. Twice. Okay, I know he didn't actually, physically kill his wife. But he may as well have done. If he'd left her, like he'd promised me, none of this would have happened.

Now, he's serving a minimum of nineteen years for the murder of his wife, and thirteen for my attempted murder. Suki only got three for being an accessory. She's up the road in Holloway. I won't be visiting *her*. That's for sure.

I pass down another corridor and through another set of gates where I'm directed to put my bag in a locker, and show my ultra-violet-stamped hand, illuminating a coat of arms on my pale skin. I tuck my hair behind my ears and smile at the officer. He nods, blank-faced, and waves me through. Copying the other visitors, I remove my coat and boots, and the cash in my jeans' pocket and place everything in a plastic tray, like I'm at the airport. I now have to submit to a body search, including my mouth where I'm made to waggle my tongue to each side. Honestly, anyone would think *I* was the criminal. I gather up my belongings, shrug my coat back on and tug my boots over my freezing feet.

We pass through one further set of ID checks before finally reaching the visitors' hall. My heart is suddenly pounding, my palms slick with sweat. Is it too late to turn back? I wipe my hands on my jeans and take a breath, scanning the room, but I don't spot him immediately. I hand my visiting order to a seated officer who checks me off against a list and then points down the hall. I follow his line of sight, past all the other seated inmates.

And there, at last, I see him… Jack. Sitting alone at a small, circular table.

My heart swoops, my stomach clenches. He's staring at me, and I can almost believe we're somewhere else. Somewhere better. In a time and place where his face would light up at the sight of me. Where he couldn't wait to kiss me and place his hands on my body.

Here, now, it doesn't feel right to smile or wave. He's already broken eye contact, his head bowed. I blink, push my shoulders back, and weave my way past the tables and chairs, past the other visitors and inmates, until, finally, I reach him.

He remains seated without acknowledging my arrival.

My heart thumps in my ears. 'Hello,' I say, but my voice is drowned out by the clatter of chair legs, and the cacophony of other prisoners greeting loved ones. 'Hi,' I say a little louder this time. He's wearing a navy sweatshirt and black jogging bottoms. His hair is still cropped short, but his face is thinner, his shoulders narrower, his eyes dull. He looks less like himself than he used to. A tear escapes from the corner of my eye. I smudge it away with my fingers. Why did he let himself end up in this place? If he'd only gone along with my plan…

'What are you doing here, Mia?' he asks, his voice leaden.

I sit opposite him, on one of the spare chairs. I suddenly can't think of anything to say. The phrase "How are you?" certainly isn't appropriate. My right eyelid twitches – a tic I haven't been able to get rid of since the summer.

He raises his eyes again to meet mine. 'I said, what are you doing here? Why did you come?'

'I'm sorry,' I finally say. 'I had to see you.'

'Was that an apology?' His lip curls into a sneer.

'I didn't want any of this to happen,' I say, aching to reach out and touch him. 'I never wanted you to end up in prison.'

'But rather me than you, eh?' He tilts his head and gives me a grim smile.

I open my mouth, but can't think of a reply.

'You and I, we know the truth, Mia, don't we?' His voice is tinged with acid. 'We know you're a liar and a murderer, even if the British justice system couldn't work out that pertinent nugget of information.'

'I…'

'You?' He raises his eyebrows. 'You *what*? You came here to gloat? To apologise? To cry?'

I swipe at another stray tear. 'You tried to kill me.'

'Yes. I did. But can you honestly blame me? You killed my wife. You were going to frame me for her murder. Is that not enough to tip any man over the edge?' He's gripping the edge of the table now, his fingers tense, white.

'I loved you,' I say. Even now, as he radiates hatred, I gaze at him and wish he loved me still. Wish he would admit that, despite everything, he still wants to be with me. I realise that's the reason I came here. To see if somehow we could make this work. But he doesn't even want to try.

'You love no one but yourself, Mia. You're sick. Deluded. Dangerous. *You* should be the one locked up. Not *me*.' His shoulders sag and he lets go his grip on the table. 'Suki was the only one who believed in me. Why couldn't you have told your precious DS Wright the truth? She would have understood. You could have explained it was an accident. They'd have gone easier on both of us.' His eyes are pleading now, bright with unshed tears. His hands are trembling. He slides them out of sight, onto his lap. 'It's not too late,' he whispers, hunching forward. 'You can turn yourself in. Please. You don't know what it's like in here. I don't know if I'll make it. Nineteen years… I can't…'

I don't want to hear this. He's sending me on another guilt trip. I came here to see if we could have a future together. To tell him I would wait for him. But he's banging on about the same old things. Accusing me, accepting none of the blame.

'You're strong,' I say. 'You'll be okay. And I can visit you again. We can—'

'No.' He shakes his head. 'I'm not strong. I'm not built for this place. I need to be back home. Back by the river. Away from this hell. Get me out of here, Mia. You're the only one who can make them believe…'

I stand up, shaken by the emotion in his voice. This was a mistake. To come here so soon. 'I'm sorry, Jack. I should go.'

'No!' his voice is too loud and we're attracting glances from the other visitors and inmates. A prison officer heads this way. I nod to let him know everything's okay, and he backs off. But he's watching closely now. Watching Jack.

'No,' Jack repeats, more quietly this time. 'Don't go. Not yet.'

I sit back down, perched on the edge of the chair. My hands clasped together.

'How can you live with yourself?' he hisses, his face flushing. 'Just tell them the truth, Mia.'

I shake my head. At this moment, he doesn't even look like the same person, his face is so twisted with rage.

'I'm sorry,' I say, standing up once more. This time I'm determined to leave.

Jack lurches to his feet, scraping his chair back. 'Tell the fucking truth!' he yells. He strides around the table towards me, his hands outstretched. The prison officers are on him in seconds, before his fingers can connect with my neck.

'Tell the truth!' he shouts as he's dragged away. 'You bitch! You lying, fucking bitch!'

Everyone is staring from him to me. Some people are laughing. My face is burning, my hands shaking, my knees like jelly. He's bundled out of the hall, through a door in the back. I lower my eyes and turn to leave.

He's still so angry. I suppose that's to be expected. But I know he'll come around, in time. He'll come back to me. And I'll be waiting for him. Because I remember everything now – my old memories and my newer amnesia memories have merged. That new Mia… she should never have existed. She was a poor imitation. A weak copy. I'm phasing her out. Overlaying her with the real me. Because after everything that's happened, I'm finally back to being myself. I finally know who I am.

A LETTER FROM SHALINI

Thank you for reading my very first thriller. I do hope you enjoyed it. My son, Dan Boland, started rowing five years ago, in the beautiful town of Christchurch, and he's absolutely hooked on it. So, I thought it would be interesting to write a story set around a fictional rowing club. Thanks, Dan, for inspiring *The Girl from the Sea*.

If you would like to keep up-to-date with my latest releases, just sign up at the link below and I'll let you know when my next novel comes out.

www.bookouture.com/shalini-boland

I'm always thrilled to get feedback about my books, so if you enjoyed it, I'd love it if you could post a short review online or tell your friends about it. Your opinion makes a huge difference helping people to discover my books for the first time.

I also love chatting to readers, so please feel free to get in touch via my *Facebook page*, through *Twitter*, *Goodreads* or my *website*.

Thanks so much!
Shalini x

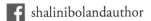 shalinibolandauthor

@shaliniboland

4727364.shalini_boland

shaliniboland.co.uk

ACKNOWLEDGEMENTS

I want to say a massive thank you to my husband, Pete Boland, for reading my first draft and giving me his encouragement and honest feedback. I'm lucky he's so supportive of my writing. He also forces me to take regular breaks, for which my mushy brain thanks him.

Thank you to my wonderful publisher Bookouture for taking on this book and breathing new life into it. And to my incredible editor Natasha Harding for her insightful comments and light touch. You are truly gifted!!

Thanks also to my original editor, Jessica Dall. Her notes were spot on. I took all her advice on board and I can't recommend her highly enough. I'd also like to thank Alexandra Holmes and Tom Feltham for their editing and proofreading skills. For catching those little things that managed to slip past everyone else's eyes.

I was lucky enough to be able to quiz two amazing police officers. I'm very grateful to Hannah Riches, an ex-detective with the Metropolitan Police. And also to Samantha Smith, an officer with the Thames Valley Police. You both rock. Any errors or embellishments in police procedure are purely my own.

I'm totally in love with my book cover and have to thank Simon Tucker from *Covered Book Designs* for creating the image that was in my head. You're a star. Thanks also to Bookouture for updating the image and bringing it in line with my other covers. It looks amazing!

I'm forever grateful to my beta readers Julie Carey and Amara Gillo who gave a clear readers' perspective. Thanks also to my fab Street Team – your support is wonderful. And to all my readers and reviewers, thank you, always.

Printed in Great Britain
by Amazon

49967054R00137